William Blake
SELECTED POEMS

COMPILED BY
PATRICIA MOORE

UNABRIGED & COMPLETE
LONG READING TEXT

NEW DELHI (INDIA)

William Blake
SELECTED
POEMS

This English Edition, Published in India

Published by

MG BOOKS

An Imprint of

MAANU GRAPHICS

MAANU GRAPHICS

(PUBLISHERS OF GENERAL BOOKS)

5FF, Ganpati Bhawan, 21 Ansari Road,
Darya Ganj, New Delhi-110002
Ph: 43755225, 9315898404
E-mail : maanugraphics@yahoo.com
mgbooks.maanu@yahoo.com

Printed at

Satyam Enterprises, Delhi

CONTENTS

About the Author

William Blake was born in London on November 28, 1757, to James, a hosier, and Catherine Blake. He learned to read and write at home. At age ten, Blake expressed a wish to become a painter, so his parents sent him to drawing school. Two years later, Blake began writing poetry. When he turned fourteen, he apprenticed with an engraver because art school proved too costly.

One of Blake's assignments as apprentice was to sketch the tombs at Westminster Abbey, exposing him to a variety of Gothic styles from which he would draw inspiration throughout his career. After his seven-year term ended, he studied briefly at the Royal Academy.

In 1782, he married an illiterate woman named Catherine Boucher. Blake taught her to read and to write, and also instructed her in draftsmanship. He believed that Robert's spirit continued to visit him and later claimed that in a dream Robert taught him the printing method that he used in Songs of Innocence and other "illuminated" works.

Blake's first printed work, Poetical Sketches (1783), is a collection of apprentice verse, mostly imitating classical models. The poems protest against war, tyranny, and King George III's treatment of the American colonies. He published his most popular collection, Songs of Innocence, in 1789 and followed it, in 1794, with Songs of Experience.

In 1800 Blake moved to the seacoast town of Felpham, where he lived and worked until 1803 under the patronage of William Hayley. He taught himself Greek, Latin, Hebrew, and Italian, so that he could read classical works in their original language.

In Felpham he experienced profound spiritual insights that prepared him for his mature work, the great visionary epics written and etched between about 1804 and 1820. Milton (1804-08), Vala, or The Four Zoas (1797; rewritten after 1800), and Jerusalem (1804-20) have neither traditional plot, characters, rhyme, nor meter. They envision a new and higher kind of innocence, the human spirit triumphant over reason.

Blake's final years, spent in great poverty, were cheered by the admiring friendship of a group of younger artists who called themselves "the Ancients."

In 1818 he met John Linnell, a young artist who helped him financially and also helped to create new interest in his work. It was Linnell who, in 1825, commissioned him to design illustrations for Dante's Divine Comedy, the cycle of drawings that Blake worked on until his death in 1827.

POETICAL SKETCHES

TO SPRING

O Thou with dewy locks, who lookest down
Thro' the clear windows of the morning, turn
Thine angel eyes upon our western isle,
Which in full choir hails thy approach, O Spring!

The hills tell each other, and the list'ning
Valleys hear; all our longing eyes are turnèd
Up to thy bright pavilions: issue forth,
And let thy holy feet visit our clime.

Come o'er the eastern hills, and let our winds
Kiss thy perfumèd garments; let us taste
Thy morn and evening breath; scatter thy pearls
Upon our love-sick land that mourns for thee.

O deck her forth with thy fair fingers; pour
Thy soft kisses on her bosom; and put
Thy golden crown upon her languish'd head,
Whose modest tresses were bound up for thee.

TO SUMMER

O thou who passest thro' our valleys in
Thy strength, curb thy fierce steeds, allay the heat
That flames from their large nostrils! thou, O Summer,
Oft pitched'st here thy golden tent, and oft

Beneath our oaks hast slept, while we beheld
With joy thy ruddy limbs and flourishing hair.
Beneath our thickest shades we oft have heard
Thy voice, when noon upon his fervid car

Rode o'er the deep of heaven; beside our springs
Sit down, and in our mossy valleys, on
Some bank beside a river clear, throw thy
Silk draperies off, and rush into the stream:
Our valleys love the Summer in his pride.
Our bards are fam'd who strike the silver wire:
Our youth are bolder than the southern swains:

Our maidens fairer in the sprightly dance:
We lack not songs, nor instruments of joy,
Nor echoes sweet, nor waters clear as heaven,
Nor laurel wreaths against the sultry heat.

TO AUTUMN

O Autumn, laden with fruit, and stainèd
With the blood of the grape, pass not, but sit

Beneath my shady roof; there thou may'st rest,
And tune thy jolly voice to my fresh pipe,

And all the daughters of the year shall dance!
Sing now the lusty song of fruits and flowers.
`The narrow bud opens her beauties to
The sun, and love runs in her thrilling veins;

Blossoms hang round the brows of Morning, and
Flourish down the bright cheek of modest Eve,
Till clust'ring Summer breaks forth into singing,
And feather'd clouds strew flowers round her head.

`The spirits of the air live on the smells
Of fruit; and Joy, with pinions light, roves round
The gardens, or sits singing in the trees.'
Thus sang the jolly Autumn as he sat;

Then rose, girded himself, and o'er the bleak
Hills fled from our sight; but left his golden load.

TO WINTER

O Winter! bar thine adamantine doors:
The north is thine; there hast thou built thy dark
Deep-founded habitation. Shake not thy roofs,
Nor bend thy pillars with thine iron car.'

He hears me not, but o'er the yawning deep
Rides heavy; his storms are unchain'd, sheathèd
In ribbèd steel; I dare not lift mine eyes,
For he hath rear'd his sceptre o'er the world.

Lo! now the direful monster, whose skin clings
To his strong bones, strides o'er the groaning rocks:
He withers all in silence, and in his hand
Unclothes the earth, and freezes up frail life.
He takes his seat upon the cliffs,- -the mariner
Cries in vain. Poor little wretch, that deal'st

With storms!- -till heaven smiles, and the monster
Is driv'n yelling to his caves beneath mount Hecla.

TO THE EVENING STAR

Thou fair-hair'd angel of the evening,
Now, whilst the sun rests on the mountains, light
Thy bright torch of love; thy radiant crown
Put on, and smile upon our evening bed!

Smile on our loves, and while thou drawest the
Blue curtains of the sky, scatter thy silver dew
On every flower that shuts its sweet eyes
In timely sleep. Let thy west wind sleep on

The lake; speak silence with thy glimmering eyes,

And wash the dusk with silver. Soon, full soon,
Dost thou withdraw; then the wolf rages wide,
And the lion glares thro' the dun forest:

The fleeces of our flocks are cover'd with
Thy sacred dew: protect them with thine influence,

TO MORNING

O holy virgin! clad in purest white,
Unlock heav'n's golden gates, and issue forth;
Awake the dawn that sleeps in heaven; let light
Rise from the chambers of the east, and bring

The honey'd dew that cometh on waking day.
O radiant morning, salute the sun
Rous'd like a huntsman to the chase, and with
Thy buskin'd feet appear upon our hills.

FAIR ELENOR

The bell struck one, and shook the silent tower;
The graves give up their dead: fair Elenor
Walk'd by the castle gate, and lookèd in.
A hollow groan ran thro' the dreary vaults.

She shriek'd aloud, and sunk upon the steps,
On the cold stone her pale cheeks. Sickly smells

Of death issue as from a sepulchre,
And all is silent but the sighing vaults.

Chill Death withdraws his hand, and she revives;
Amaz'd, she finds herself upon her feet,
And, like a ghost, thro' narrow passages
Walking, feeling the cold walls with her hands.

Fancy returns, and now she thinks of bones
And grinning skulls, and corruptible death
Wrapp'd in his shroud; and now fancies she hears
Deep sighs, and sees pale sickly ghosts gliding.

At length, no fancy but reality
Distracts her. A rushing sound, and the feet
Of one that fled, approaches- -Ellen stood
Like a dumb statue, froze to stone with fear.

The wretch approaches, crying: `The deed is done;
Take this, and send it by whom thou wilt send;
It is my life- -send it to Elenor:- -
He's dead, and howling after me for blood!

`Take this,' he cried; and thrust into her arms
A wet napkin, wrapp'd about; then rush'd
Past, howling: she receiv'd into her arms
Pale death, and follow'd on the wings of fear.

They pass'd swift thro' the outer gate; the wretch,
Howling, leap'd o'er the wall into the moat,
Stifling in mud. Fair Ellen pass'd the bridge,
And heard a gloomy voice cry `Is it done?'

As the deer wounded, Ellen flew over
The pathless plain; as the arrows that fly
By night, destruction flies, and strikes in darkness.
She fled from fear, till at her house arriv'd.

Her maids await her; on her bed she falls,
That bed of joy, where erst her lord hath press'd:
`Ah, woman's fear!' she cried; `ah, cursèd duke!
Ah, my dear lord! ah, wretched Elenor!

`My lord was like a flower upon the brows
Of lusty May! Ah, life as frail as flower!
O ghastly death! withdraw thy cruel hand,
Seek'st thou that flow'r to deck thy horrid temples?

`My lord was like a star in highest heav'n
Drawn down to earth by spells and wickedness;
My lord was like the opening eyes of day

When western winds creep softly o'er the flowers;
`But he is darken'd; like the summer's noon
Clouded; fall'n like the stately tree, cut down;
The breath of heaven dwelt among his leaves.

O Elenor, weak woman, fill'd with woe!'
Thus having spoke, she raisèd up her head,
And saw the bloody napkin by her side,
Which in her arms she brought; and now, tenfold

More terrifièd, saw it unfold itself.
Her eyes were fix'd; the bloody cloth unfolds,
Disclosing to her sight the murder'd head
Of her dear lord, all ghastly pale, clotted

With gory blood; it groan'd, and thus it spake:
`O Elenor, I am thy husband's head,
Who, sleeping on the stones of yonder tower,
Was 'reft of life by the accursèd duke!

A hirèd villain turn'd my sleep to death!
`O Elenor, beware the cursèd duke;
O give not him thy hand, now I am dead;
He seeks thy love; who, coward, in the night,

Hirèd a villain to bereave my life.'
She sat with dead cold limbs, stiffen'd to stone;
She took the gory head up in her arms;
She kiss'd the pale lips; she had no tears to shed;
She hugg'd it to her breast, and groan'd her last.

SONG

How sweet I roam'd from field to field
And tasted all the summer's pride,
Till I the Prince of Love beheld
Who in the sunny beams did glide!

He show'd me lilies for my hair,
And blushing roses for my brow;
He led me through his gardens fair
Where all his golden pleasures grow.

With sweet May dews my wings were wet,
And Phoebus fir'd my vocal rage;
He caught me in his silken net,
And shut me in his golden cage.

He loves to sit and hear me sing,
Then, laughing, sports and plays with me;
Then stretches out my golden wing,
And mocks my loss of liberty.

SONG

My silks and fine array,
My smiles and languish'd air,
By love are driv'n away;
And mournful lean Despair

Brings me yew to deck my grave;
Such end true lovers have.
His face is fair as heav'n
When springing buds unfold;

O why to him was't giv'n
Whose heart is wintry cold?
His breast is love's all-worshipp'd tomb,
Where all love's pilgrims come.

Bring me an axe and spade,
Bring me a winding-sheet
When I my grave have made
Let winds and tempests beat:

Then down I'll lie as cold as clay.
True love doth pass away!

SONG

Love and harmony combine,
And around our souls entwine
While thy branches mix with mine,
And our roots together join.

Joys upon our branches sit,
Chirping loud and singing sweet;
Like gentle streams beneath our feet
Innocence and virtue meet.

Thou the golden fruit dost bear,
I am clad in flowers fair;
Thy sweet boughs perfume the air,
And the turtle buildeth there.
There she sits and feeds her young,

Sweet I hear her mournful song;
And thy lovely leaves among,
There is love, I hear his tongue.
There his charming nest doth lay,

There he sleeps the night away;
There he sports along the day,
And doth among our branches play.

SONG

I love the jocund dance,
The softly breathing song,
Where innocent eyes do glance,
And where lisps the maiden's tongue.

I love the laughing vale,
I love the echoing hill,
Where mirth does never fail,
And the jolly swain laughs his fill.

I love the pleasant cot,
I love the innocent bow'r,
Where white and brown is our lot,
Or fruit in the mid-day hour.

I love the oaken seat,
Beneath the oaken tree,
Where all the old villagers meet,
And laugh our sports to see.

I love our neighbours all,
But, Kitty, I better love thee;
And love them I ever shall;
But thou art all to me.

SONG

Memory, hither come
And tune your merry notes
And, while upon the wind
Your music floats,

I'll pore upon the stream
Where sighing lovers dream,
And fish for fancies as they pass
Within the watery glass.

I'll drink of the clear stream,

And hear the linnet's song;
And there I'll lie and dream
The day along:

And when night comes, I'll go
To places fit for woe,
Walking along the darken'd valley
With silent Melancholy.

MAD SONG

The wild winds weep,
And the night is a-cold;
Come hither, Sleep,
And my griefs unfold:

But lo! the morning peeps
Over the eastern steeps,
And the rustling beds of dawn
The earth do scorn.

Lo! to the vault
Of pavèd heaven,
With sorrow fraught
My notes are driven:

They strike the ear of night,
Make weep the eyes of day;

They make made the roaring winds,
And with tempests play.

Like a fiend in a cloud,
With howling woe
After night I do crowd,
And with night will go;

I turn my back to the east
From whence comforts have increas'd
For light doth seize my brain
With frantic pain.

SONG

Fresh from the dewy hill, the merry year
Smiles on my head and mounts his flaming car;
Round my young brows the laurel wreathes a shade,
And rising glories beam around my head.

My feet are wing'd, while o'er the dewy lawn,
I meet my maiden risen like the morn:
O bless those holy feet, like angels' feet;
O bless those limbs, beaming with heav'nly light.

Like as an angel glitt'ring in the sky
In times of innocence and holy joy;
The joyful shepherd stops his grateful song
To hear the music of an angel's tongue.

So when she speaks, the voice of Heaven I hear;
So when we walk, nothing impure comes near;
Each field seems Eden, and each calm retreat;
Each village seems the haunt of holy feet.

But that sweet village where my black-eyed maid
Closes her eyes in sleep beneath night's shade,
Whene'er I enter, more than mortal fire
Burns in my soul, and does my song inspire.

SONG

When early morn walks forth in sober grey,
Then to my black-eyed maid I haste away;
When evening sits beneath her dusky bow'r,
And gently sighs away the silent hour,

The village bell alarms, away I go,
And the vale darkens at my pensive woe.
To that sweet village, where my black-eyed maid
Doth drop a tear beneath the silent shade,

I turn my eyes; and pensive as I go
Curse my black stars and bless my pleasing woe.
Oft when the summer sleeps among the trees,
Whisp'ring faint murmurs to the scanty breeze,

I walk the village round; if at her side
A youth doth walk in stolen joy and pride,
I curse my stars in bitter grief and woe,
That made my love so high and me so low.

O should she e'er prove false, his limbs I'd tear
And throw all pity on the burning air;
I'd curse bright fortune for my mixèd lot,
And then I'd die in peace and be forgot.

TO THE MUSES

Whether on Ida's shady brow,
Or in the chambers of the East,
The chambers of the sun, that now
From ancient melody have ceas'd;

Whether in Heaven ye wander fair,
Or the green corners of the earth,
Or the blue regions of the air
Where the melodious winds have birth;

Whether on crystal rocks ye rove,
Beneath the bosom of the sea
Wand'ring in many a coral grove,
Fair Nine, forsaking Poetry!

How have you left the ancient love
That bards of old enjoy'd in you!

The languid strings do scarcely move!
The sound is forc'd, the notes are few

GWIN KING OF NORWAY

Come, kings, and listen to my song:
When Gwin, the son of Nore,
Over the nations of the North

His cruel sceptre bore;
The nobles of the land did feed
Upon the hungry poor;
They tear the poor man's lamb, and drive

The needy from their door.
`The land is desolate; our wives
And children cry for bread;
Arise, and pull the tyrant down!

Let Gwin be humblèd!'
Gordred the giant rous'd himself
From sleeping in his cave;
He shook the hills, and in the clouds

The troubl'd banners wave.
Beneath them roll'd, like tempests black,
The num'rous sons of blood;
Like lions' whelps, roaring abroad,

Seeking their nightly food.
Down Bleron's hills they dreadful rush,
Their cry ascends the clouds;
The trampling horse and clanging arms
Like rushing mighty floods!

Their wives and children, weeping loud,
Follow in wild array,
Howling like ghosts, furious as wolves
In the bleak wintry day.

`Pull down the tyrant to the dust,
Let Gwin be humblèd,'
They cry, `and let ten thousand lives
Pay for the tyrant's head.'

From tow'r to tow'r the watchmen cry,
`O Gwin, the son of Nore,
Arouse thyself! the nations, black
Like clouds, come rolling o'er!'

Gwin rear'd his shield, his palace shakes,
His chiefs come rushing round;
Each, like an awful thunder cloud,
With voice of solemn sound:

Like rearèd stones around a grave
They stand around the King;
Then suddenly each seiz'd his spear,
And clashing steel does ring.

The husbandman does leave his plough
To wade thro' fields of gore;
The merchant binds his brows in steel,
And leaves the trading shore;

The shepherd leaves his mellow pipe,
And sounds the trumpet shrill;
The workman throws his hammer down
To heave the bloody bill.

Like the tall ghost of Barraton
Who sports in stormy sky,
Gwin leads his host, as black as night
When pestilence does fly,

With horses and with chariots- -
And all his spearmen bold
March to the sound of mournful song,
Like clouds around him roll'd.
Gwin lifts his hand- -the nations halt;

`Prepare for war!' he cries- -
Gordred appears!- -his frowning brow
Troubles our northern skies.
The armies stand, like balances

Held in th' Almighty's hand;- -
`Gwin, thou hast fill'd thy measure up:
Thou'rt swept from out the land.'
And now the raging armies rush'd

Like warring mighty seas;
The heav'ns are shook with roaring war,
The dust ascends the skies!
Earth smokes with blood, and groans and shakes

To drink her children's gore,
A sea of blood; nor can the eye
See to the trembling shore!
And on the verge of this wild sea

Famine and death doth cry;
The cries of women and of babes
Over the field doth fly.
The King is seen raging afar,

With all his men of might;
Like blazing comets scattering death

Thro' the red fev'rous night.
Beneath his arm like sheep they die,

And groan upon the plain;
The battle faints, and bloody men
Fight upon hills of slain.
Now death is sick, and riven men

Labour and toil for life;
Steed rolls on steed, and shield on shield,
Sunk in this sea of strife!
The god of war is drunk with blood;

The earth doth faint and fail;
The stench of blood makes sick the heav'ns;
Ghosts glut the throat of hell!
O what have kings to answer for
Before that awful throne;
When thousand deaths for vengeance cry,
And ghosts accusing groan!

Like blazing comets in the sky
That shake the stars of light,
Which drop like fruit unto the earth
Thro' the fierce burning night;
Like these did Gwin and Gordred meet,
And the first blow decides;
Down from the brow unto the breast

Gordred his head divides!

Gwin fell: the sons of Norway fled,
All that remain'd alive;
The rest did fill the vale of death,
For them the eagles strive.
The river Dorman roll'd their blood
Into the northern sea;
Who mourn'd his sons, and overwhelm'd
The pleasant south country.

An Imitation of Spenser
Golden Apollo, that thro' heaven wide
Scatter'st the rays of light, and truth's beams,
In lucent words my darkling verses dight,
And wash my earthy mind in thy clear streams,
That wisdom may descend in fairy dreams,
All while the jocund hours in thy train

Scatter their fancies at thy poet's feet;
And when thou yields to night thy wide domain,
Let rays of truth enlight his sleeping brain.

For brutish Pan in vain might thee assay
With tinkling sounds to dash thy nervous verse,
Sound without sense; yet in his rude affray,
(For ignorance is Folly's leasing nurse
And love of Folly needs none other's curse)

Midas the praise hath gain'd of lengthen'd ears,
For which himself might deem him ne'er the worse
To sit in council with his modern peers,
And judge of tinkling rimes and elegances terse.
And thou, Mercurius, that with wingèd brow
Dost mount aloft into the yielding sky,

And thro' Heav'n's halls thy airy flight dost throw,
Entering with holy feet to where on high
Jove weighs the counsel of futurity;
Then, laden with eternal fate, dost go
Down, like a falling star, from autumn sky,
And o'er the surface of the silent deep dost fly:

If thou arrivest at the sandy shore
Where nought but envious hissing adders dwell,
Thy golden rod, thrown on the dusty floor,
Can charm to harmony with potent spell.
Such is sweet Eloquence, that does dispel
Envy and Hate that thirst for human gore;
And cause in sweet society to dwell
Vile savage minds that lurk in lonely cell

O Mercury, assist my lab'ring sense
That round the circle of the world would fly,
As the wing'd eagle scorns the tow'ry fence
Of Alpine hills round his high aëry,
And searches thro' the corners of the sky,

Sports in the clouds to hear the thunder's sound,
And see the wingèd lightnings as they fly;
Then, bosom'd in an amber cloud, around
Plumes his wide wings, and seeks Sol's palace high.

And thou, O warrior maid invincible,
Arm'd with the terrors of Almighty Jove,
Pallas, Minerva, maiden terrible,
Lov'st thou to walk the peaceful solemn grove,
In solemn gloom of branches interwove?
Or bear'st thy AEgis o'er the burning field,
Where, like the sea, the waves of battle move?
Or have thy soft piteous eyes beheld
The weary wanderer thro' the desert rove?
Or does th' afflicted man thy heav'nly bosom move?

BLIND MAN'S BUFF

When silver snow decks Susan's clothes,
And jewel hangs at th' shepherd's nose,
The blushing bank is all my care,
With hearth so red, and walls so fair;
`Heap the sea-coal, come, heap it higher,
The oaken log lay on the fire.'
The well-wash'd stools, a circling row,
With lad and lass, how fair the show!
The merry can of nut-brown ale,
The laughing jest, the love-sick tale,

Till, tir'd of chat, the game begins.
The lasses prick the lads with pins;
Roger from Dolly twitch'd the stool,
She, falling, kiss'd the ground, poor fool!
She blush'd so red, with sidelong glance
At hob-nail Dick, who griev'd the chance.
But now for Blind man's Buff they call;
Of each encumbrance clear the hall- -
Jenny her silken 'kerchief folds,
And blear-eyed Will the black lot holds.
Now laughing stops, with `Silence! hush!'
And Peggy Pout gives Sam a push.
The Blind man's arms, extended wide,
Sam slips between:- -`O woe betide
Thee, clumsy Will!'- -but titt'ring Kate
Is penn'd up in the corner straight!
And now Will's eyes beheld the play;
He thought his face was t'other way.
`Now, Kitty, now! what chance hast thou,
Roger so near thee!- -Trips, I vow!'
She catches him- -then Roger ties
His own head up- -but not his eyes;
For thro' the slender cloth he sees,
And runs at Sam, who slips with ease
His clumsy hold; and, dodging round,
Sukey is tumbled on the ground!- -
`See what it is to play unfair!

Where cheating is, there's mischief there.'
But Roger still pursues the chase,- -
`He sees! he sees!' cries, softly, Grace;
`O Roger, thou, unskill'd in art,
Must, surer bound, go thro' thy part!'
Now Kitty, pert, repeats the rimes,
And Roger turns him round three times,
Then pauses ere he starts- -but Dick
Was mischief bent upon a trick;
Down on his hands and knees he lay
Directly in the Blind man's way,
Then cries out `Hem!' Hodge heard, and ran
With hood-wink'd chance- -sure of his man;
But down he came. - - Alas, how frail
Our best of hopes, how soon they fail!
With crimson drops he stains the ground;
Confusion startles all around.
Poor piteous Dick supports his head,
And fain would cure the hurt he made.
But Kitty hasted with a key,
And down his back they straight convey
The cold relief; the blood is stay'd,
And Hodge again holds up his head.
Such are the fortunes of the game,
And those who play should stop the same
By wholesome laws; such as all those
Who on the blinded man impose
Stand in his stead; as, long a-gone,

When men were first a nation grown,
Lawless they liv'd, till wantonness
And liberty began t' increase,
And one man lay in another's way;
Then laws were made to keep fair play.

APPENDIX TO POETICAL SKETCHES

SONG BY A SHEPHERD

Welcome, stranger, to this place,
Where joy doth sit on every bough,
Paleness flies from every face;
We reap not what we do not sow.
Innocence doth like a rose
Bloom on every maiden's cheek;
Honour twines around her brows,
The jewel health adorns her neck.

SONG BY AN OLD SHEPHERD

When silver snow decks Sylvio's clothes,
And jewel hangs at shepherd's nose,
We can abide life's pelting storm,
That makes our limbs quake, if our hearts be warm.
Whilst Virtue is our walking-staff,
And Truth a lantern to our path,
We can abide life's pelting storm,
That makes our limbs quake, if our hearts be warm.

Blow, boisterous wind, stern winter frown,
Innocence is a winter's gown.
So clad, we'll abide life's pelting storm,
That makes our limbs quake, if our hearts be warm.

SONGS FROM AN ISLAND IN THE MOON

I

Little Phoebus came strutting in,
With his fat belly and his round chin.
What is it you would please to have?
Ho! Ho!
I won't let it go at only so and so!

II

Honour and Genius is all I ask,
And I ask the Gods no more!
No more! No more!
No more! No more!} The Three Philosophers bear chorus.

III

When Old Corruption first begun,
Adorn'd in yellow vest,

He committed on Flesh a whoredom - -
O, what a wicked beast!
From then a callow babe did spring,
And Old Corruption smil'd
To think his race should never end,
For now he had a child.
He call'd him Surgery and fed
The babe with his own milk;
For Flesh and he could ne'er agree:
She would not let him suck.
And this he always kept in mind;
And form'd a crooked knife,
And ran about with bloody hands
To seek his mother's life.
And as he ran to seek his mother
He met with a dead woman.
He fell in love and married her - -
A deed which is not common!
She soon grew pregnant, and brought forth
Scurvy and Spotted Fever,
The father grinn'd and skipt about,
And said `I'm made for ever!
`For now I have procur'd these imps
I'll try experiments.'
With that he tied poor Scurvy down,
And stopt up all its vents.
And when the child began to swell
He shouted out aloud - -

`I've found the dropsy out, and soon
Shall do the world more good.'
He took up Fever by the neck,
And cut out all its spots;
And, thro' the holes which he had made,
He first discover'd guts.

IV

Hear then the pride and knowledge of a sailor!
His sprit sail, fore sail, main sail, and his mizen.
A poor frail man - - God wot! I know none frailer,
I know no greater sinner than John Taylor.

V

The Song of Phoebe and Jellicoe
Phoebe drest like beauty's queen,
Jellicoe in faint pea-green,
Sitting all beneath a grot,
Where the little lambkins trot.
Maidens dancing, loves a-sporting,
All the country folks a-courting,
Susan, Johnny, Bob, and Joe,
Lightly tripping on a row.
Happy people, who can be
In happiness compar'd with ye?
The pilgrim with his crook and hat
Sees your happiness complete.

VI

Lo! the Bat with leathern wing,
Winking and blinking,
Winking and blinking,
Winking and blinking,
Like Dr Johnson.
Quid. `O ho!' said Dr. Johnson
To Scipio Africanus,
Suction. `A ha!' to Dr. Johnson
Said Scipio Africanus,
And the Cellar goes down with a step. (Grand Chorus.)

VII

1st Vo. Want Matches?
2nd Vo. Yes! Yes! Yes!
1st Vo. Want Matches?
2nd Vo. No!
1st Vo. Want Matches?
2nd Vo. Yes! Yes! Yes!
1st Vo Want Matches?
2nd Vo. No!

VIII

As I walk'd forth one May morning
To see the fields so pleasant and so gay,
O! there did I spy a young maiden sweet,
Among the violets that smell so sweet,
smell so sweet,

smell so sweet,
Among the violets that smell so sweet.

IX

Hail Matrimony, made of Love!
To thy wide gates how great a drove
On purpose to be yok'd do come;
Widows and Maids and Youths also,
That lightly trip on beauty's toe,
Or sit on beauty's bum.
Hail fingerfooted lovely Creatures!
The females of our human natures,
Formèd to suckle all Mankind.
'Tis you that come in time of need,
Without you we should never breed,
Or any comfort find.
For if a Damsel's blind or lame,
Or Nature's hand has crook'd her frame,
Or if she's deaf, or is wall-eyed;
Yet, if her heart is well inclin'd,
Some tender lover she shall find
That panteth for a Bride.
The universal Poultice this,
To cure whatever is amiss
In Damsel or in Widow gay!
It makes them smile, it makes them skip;
Like birds, just curèd of the pip,
They chirp and hop away.

Then come, ye maidens! come, ye swains!
Come and be cur'd of all your pains
In Matrimony's Golden Cage - -

X

To be or not to be
Of great capacity,
Like Sir Isaac Newton,
Or Locke, or Doctor South,
Or Sherlock upon Death - -
I'd rather be Sutton!
For he did build a house
For agèd men and youth,
With walls of brick and stone;
He furnish'd it within
With whatever he could win,
And all his own.
He drew out of the Stocks
His money in a box,
And sent his servant
To Green the Bricklayer,
And to the Carpenter;
He was so fervent.
The chimneys were threescore,
The windows many more;
And, for convenience,
He sinks and gutters made,
And all the way he pav'd

To hinder pestilence.
Was not this a good man - -
Whose life was but a span,
Whose name was Sutton - -
As Locke, or Doctor South,
Or Sherlock upon Death,
Or Sir Isaac Newton?

XI

This city and this country has brought forth many mayors
To sit in state, and give forth laws out' of their old oak chairs,
With face as brown as any nut with drinking of strong ale - -
Good English hospitality, O then it did not fail!
With scarlet gowns and broad gold lace, would make a yeoman sweat;
With stockings roll'd above their knees and shoes as black as jet
With eating beef and drinking beer, O they were stout and hale - -
Good English hospitality, O then it did not fail!
Thus sitting at the table wide the mayor and aldermen
Were fit to give law to the city; each ate as much as ten:
The hungry poor enter'd the hall to eat good beef and ale - -
Good English hospitality, O then it did not fail!

XII

O, I say, you Joe,
Throw us the ball!
I've a good mind to go
And leave you all.
I never saw such a bowler
To bowl the ball in a tansy,
And to clean it with my hankercher
Without saying a word.
That Bill's a foolish fellow;
He has given me a black eye.
He does not know how to handle a bat
Any more than a dog or a cat:
He has knock'd down the wicket,
And broke the stumps,
And runs without shoes to save his pumps.

XIII

Leave, O leave me to my sorrows;
Here I'll sit and fade away,
Till I'm nothing but a spirit,
And I lose this form of clay.
Then if chance along this forest
Any walk in pathless ways,
Thro' the gloom he'll see my shadow
Hear my voice upon the breeze.

XIV

There's Doctor Clash,
And Signor Falalasole,
O they sweep in the cash
Into their purse hole!
Fa me la sol, La me fa sol!
Great A, little A,
Bouncing B!
Play away, play away,
You're out of the key!
Fa me la sol, La me fa sol!
Musicians should have
A pair of very good ears,
And long fingers and thumbs,
And not like clumsy bears.
Fa me la sol, La me fa sol!
Gentlemen! Gentlemen!
Rap! Rap! Rap!
Fiddle! Fiddle! Fiddle!
Clap! Clap! Clap!
Fa me la sol, La me fa sol!

SONGS OF INNOCENCE

INTRODUCTION

Piping down the valleys wild,
Piping songs of pleasant glee,
On a cloud I saw a child,
And he laughing said to me:

`Pipe a song about a Lamb!'
So I piped with merry cheer.
`Piper, pipe that song again;'
So I piped: he wept to hear.

`Drop thy pipe, thy happy pipe;
Sing thy songs of happy cheer:'
So I sang the same again,
While he wept with joy to hear.

`Piper, sit thee down and write
In a book, that all may read.'
So he vanish'd from my sight,
And I pluck'd a hollow reed,

And I made a rural pen,
And I stain'd the water clear,
And I wrote my happy songs
Every child may joy to hear.

THE ECHOING GREEN

The Sun does arise,
And make happy the skies;
The merry bells ring
To welcome the Spring;

The skylark and thrush,
The birds of the bush,
Sing louder around
To the bells' cheerful sound,

While our sports shall be seen
On the Echoing Green.
Old John, with white hair,
Does laugh away care,

Sitting under the oak,
Among the old folk.
They laugh at our play,
And soon they all say:

`Such, such were the joys
When we all, girls and boys,

In our youth time were seen
On the Echoing Green.'

Till the little ones, weary,
No more can be merry;
The sun does descend,
And our sports have an end.

Round the laps of their mothers
Many sisters and brothers,
Like birds in their nest,
Are ready for rest,

And sport no more seen
On the darkening Green.

THE LAMB

Little Lamb, who made thee?
Dost thou know who made thee?
Gave thee life, and bid thee feed,
By the stream and o'er the mead;
Gave thee clothing of delight,
Softest clothing, woolly, bright;
Gave thee such a tender voice,
Making all the vales rejoice?
Little Lamb, who made thee?
Dost thou know who made thee?

Little Lamb, I'll tell thee,
Little Lamb, I'll tell thee:
He is callèd by thy name,
For He calls Himself a Lamb.
He is meek, and He is mild;
He became a little child.
I a child, and thou a lamb,
We are callèd by His name.
Little Lamb, God bless thee!
Little Lamb, God bless thee!

THE SHEPHERD

How sweet is the Shepherd's sweet lot!
From the morn to the evening he strays;
He shall follow his sheep all the day,
And his tongue shall be fillèd with praise.
For he hears the lamb's innocent call,
And he hears the ewe's tender reply;
He is watchful while they are in peace,
For they know when their Shepherd is nigh.

INFANT JOY

`I have no name:
I am but two days old.'
What shall I call thee?
`I happy am,

Joy is my name.'
Sweet joy befall thee!
Pretty Joy!
Sweet Joy, but two days old.
Sweet Joy I call thee
Thou dost smile,
I sing the while,
Sweet joy befall thee!

THE LITTLE BLACK BOY

My mother bore me in the southern wild,
And I am black, but O! my soul is white;
White as an angel is the English child,
But I am black, as if bereav'd of light.

My mother taught me underneath a tree,
And, sitting down before the heat of day,
She took me on her lap and kissèd me,
And, pointing to the east, began to say:

`Look on the rising sun, - - there God does live,
And gives His light, and gives His heat away;
And flowers and trees and beasts and men receive
Comfort in morning, joy in the noonday.

`And we are put on earth a little space,
That we may learn to bear the beams of love;

And these black bodies and this sunburnt face
Is but a cloud, and like a shady grove,

`For when our souls have learn'd the heat to bear,
The cloud will vanish; we shall hear His voice,
Saying: "Come out from the grove, My love and care,
And round My golden tent like lambs rejoice."'

Thus did my mother say, and kissèd me;
And thus I say to little English boy.
When I from black and he from white cloud free,
And round the tent of God like lambs we joy,

I'll shade him from the heat, till he can bear
To lean in joy upon our Father's knee;
And then I'll stand and stroke his silver hair,
And be like him, and he will then love me.

LAUGHING SONG

When the green woods laugh with the voice of joy,
And the dimpling stream runs laughing by;
When the air does laugh with our merry wit,
And the green hill laughs with the noise of it;

When the meadows laugh with lively green,
And the grasshopper laughs in the merry scene,
When Mary and Susan and Emily

With their sweet round mouths sing `Ha, Ha, He!'

When the painted birds laugh in the shade,
Where our table with cherries and nuts is spread,
Come live, and be merry, and join with me,
To sing the sweet chorus of `Ha, Ha, He!'

SPRING

Sound the flute!
Now it's mute.
Birds delight
Day and night;
Nightingale
In the dale,
Lark in sky,
Merrily,
Merrily, merrily, to welcome in the year.
Little boy,
Full of joy;
Little girl,
Sweet and small;
Cock does crow,
So do you;
Merry voice,
Infant noise,
Merrily, merrily, to welcome in the year.
Little lamb,

Here I am;
Come and lick
My white neck;
Let me pull
Your soft wool;
Let me kiss
Your soft face:
Merrily, merrily, we welcome in the year.

A CRADLE SONG

Sweet dreams, form a shade
O'er my lovely infant's head;
Sweet dreams of pleasant streams
By happy, silent, moony beams.

Sweet sleep, with soft down
Weave thy brows an infant crown.
Sweet sleep, Angel mild,
Hover o'er my happy child.

Sweet smiles, in the night
Hover over my delight;
Sweet smiles, mother's smiles,
All the livelong night beguiles.

Sweet moans, dovelike sighs,
Chase not slumber from thy eyes.

Sweet moans, sweeter smiles,
All the dovelike moans beguiles.

Sleep, sleep, happy child,
All creation slept and smil'd;
Sleep, sleep, happy sleep,
While o'er thee thy mother weep.

Sweet babe, in thy face
Holy image I can trace.
Sweet babe, once like thee,
Thy Maker lay and wept for me,

Wept for me, for thee, for all,
When He was an infant small.
Thou His image ever see,
Heavenly face that smiles on thee

Smiles on thee, on me, on all;
Who became an infant small.
Infant smiles are His own smiles;
Heaven and earth to peace beguiles.

NURSE'S SONG

When the voices of children are heard on the green,
And laughing is heard on the hill,
My heart is at rest within my breast,

And everything else is still.

`Then come home, my children, the sun is gone down,
And the dews of night arise;
Come, come leave off play, and let us away
Till the morning appears in the skies.'

`No, no, let us play, for it is yet day,
And we cannot go to sleep;
Besides, in the sky the little birds fly,
And the hills are all cover'd with sheep.'

`Well, well, go and play till the light fades away,
And then go home to bed.'
The little ones leapèd and shoutèd and laugh'd
And all the hills echoèd.

HOLY THURSDAY

'Twas on a Holy Thursday, their innocent faces clean,
The children walking two and two, in red and blue and green,
Grey-headed beadles walk'd before, with wands as white as snow,
Till into the high dome of Paul's they like Thames' waters flow.

O what a multitude they seem'd, these flowers of London town!

Seated in companies they sit with radiance all their own.

The hum of multitudes was there, but multitudes of lambs,

Thousands of little boys and girls raising their innocent hands.

Now like a mighty wind they raise to Heaven the voice of song,

Or like harmonious thunderings the seats of Heaven among.

Beneath them sit the aged men, wise guardians of the poor;

Then cherish pity, lest you drive an angel from your door.

THE BLOSSOM

Merry, merry sparrow!
Under leaves so green,
A happy blossom
Sees you, swift as arrow,
Seek your cradle narrow
Near my bosom.
Pretty, pretty robin!
Under leaves so green,
A happy blossom
Hears you sobbing, sobbing,
Pretty, pretty robin,
Near my bosom.

THE CHIMNEY SWEEPER

When my mother died I was very young,
And my father sold me while yet my tongue
Could scarcely cry `'weep! 'weep! 'weep! 'weep!'
So your chimneys I sweep, and in soot I sleep.
There's little Tom Dacre, who cried when his head,
That curl'd like a lamb's back, was shav'd: so I said
`Hush, Tom! never mind it, for when your head's bare
You know that the soot cannot spoil your white hair.'
And so he was quiet, and that very night,
As Tom was a-sleeping, he had such a sight!- -
That thousands of sweepers, Dick, Joe, Ned, and Jack,
Were all of them lock'd up in coffins of black.
And by came an Angel who had a bright key,
And he open'd the coffins and set them all free;
Then down a green plain leaping, laughing, they run,
And wash in a river, and shine in the sun.
Then naked and white, all their bags left behind,
They rise upon clouds and sport in the wind;
And the Angel told Tom, if he'd be a good boy,
He'd have God for his father, and never want joy.
And so Tom awoke; and we rose in the dark,
And got with our bags and our brushes to work.
Tho' the morning was cold, Tom was happy and warm;
So if all do their duty they need not fear harm.

THE DIVINE IMAGE

To Mercy, Pity, Peace, and Love
All pray in their distress;
And to these virtues of delight
Return their thankfulness.

For Mercy, Pity, Peace, and Love
Is God, our Father dear,
And Mercy, Pity, Peace, and Love
Is man, His child and care.

For Mercy has a human heart,
Pity a human face,
And Love, the human form divine,
And Peace, the human dress.

Then every man, of every clime,
That prays in his distress,
Prays to the human form divine,
Love, Mercy, Pity, Peace.

And all must love the human form,
In heathen, Turk, or Jew;
Where Mercy, Love, and Pity dwell
There God is dwelling too.

NIGHT

The sun descending in the west,
The evening star does shine;
The birds are silent in their nest,
And I must seek for mine.

The moon, like a flower,
In heaven's high bower,
With silent delight
Sits and smiles on the night.

Farewell, green fields and happy groves,
Where flocks have took delight.
Where lambs have nibbled, silent moves
The feet of angels bright;

Unseen they pour blessing,
And joy without ceasing,
On each bud and blossom,
And each sleeping bosom.

They look in every thoughtless nest,
Where birds are cover'd warm;
They visit caves of every beast,
To keep them all from harm.

If they see any weeping
That should have been sleeping,

They pour sleep on their head,
And sit down by their bed.

When wolves and tigers howl for prey,
They pitying stand and weep;
Seeking to drive their thirst away,
And keep them from the sheep.

But if they rush dreadful,
The angels, most heedful,
Receive each mild spirit,
New worlds to inherit.

And there the lion's ruddy eyes
Shall flow with tears of gold,
And pitying the tender cries,
And walking round the fold,

Saying `Wrath, by His meekness,
And, by His health, sickness
Is driven away
From our immortal day.

`And now beside thee, bleating lamb,
I can lie down and sleep;
Or think on Him who bore thy name,
Graze after thee and weep.

For, wash'd in life's river.
My bright mane for ever
Shall shine like the gold
As I guard o'er the fold.'

A DREAM

Once a dream did weave a shade
O'er my Angel-guarded bed,
That an emmet lost its way
Where on grass methought I lay.

Troubled, 'wilder'd, and forlorn,
Dark, benighted, travel-worn,
Over many a tangled spray,
All heart-broke I heard her say:

`O, my children! do they cry?
Do they hear their father sigh?
Now they look abroad to see:
Now return and weep for me.'

Pitying, I dropp'd a tear;
But I saw a glow-worm near,
Who replied: `What wailing wight
Calls the watchman of the night?

`I am set to light the ground,
While the beetle goes his round:

Follow now the beetle's hum;
Little wanderer, hie thee home.'

ON ANOTHER'S SORROW

Can I see another's woe,
And not be in sorrow too?
Can I see another's grief,
And not seek for kind relief?

Can I see a falling tear,
And not feel my sorrow's share?
Can a father see his child
Weep, nor be with sorrow fill'd?

Can a mother sit and hear
An infant groan, an infant fear?
No, no! never can it be!
Never, never can it be!

And can He who smiles on all
Hear the wren with sorrows small,
Hear the small bird's grief and care,
Hear the woes that infants bear,

And not sit beside the nest,
Pouring pity in their breast;
And not sit the cradle near,

Weeping tear on infant's tear;

And not sit both night and day,
Wiping all our tears away?
O, no! never can it be!
Never, never can it be!

He doth give His joy to all;
He becomes an infant small;
He becomes a man of woe;
He doth feel the sorrow too.

Think not thou canst sigh a sigh,
And thy Maker is not by;
Think not thou canst weep a tear,
And thy Maker is not near.

O! He gives to us His joy
That our grief He may destroy;
Till our grief is fled and gone
He doth sit by us and moan.

THE LITTLE BOY LOST

`Father! father! where are you going?
O do not walk so fast.
Speak, father, speak to your little boy,
Or else I shall be lost.'

The night was dark, no father was there;
The child was wet with dew;
The mire was deep, and the child did weep,
And away the vapour flew.

THE LITTLE BOY FOUND

The little boy lost in the lonely fen,
Led by the wand'ring light,
Began to cry; but God, ever nigh,
Appear'd like his father, in white.

He kissèd the child, and by the hand led,
And to his mother brought,
Who in sorrow pale, thro' the lonely dale,
Her little boy weeping sought.

SONGS OF EXPERIENCE

INTRODUCTION

Hear the voice of the Bard!
Who present, past, and future, sees;
Whose ears have heard
The Holy Word
That walk'd among the ancient trees,

Calling the lapsèd soul,
And weeping in the evening dew;
That might control
The starry pole,
And fallen, fallen light renew!

`O Earth, O Earth, return!
Arise from out the dewy grass;
Night is worn,
And the morn
Rises from the slumberous mass.

`Turn away no more;
Why wilt thou turn away.

The starry floor,
The wat'ry shore,
Is giv'n thee till the break of day.'

EARTH'S ANSWER

Earth rais'd up her head
From the darkness dread and drear.
Her light fled,
Stony dread!
And her locks cover'd with grey despair.

`Prison'd on wat'ry shore,
Starry Jealousy does keep my den:
Cold and hoar,
Weeping o'er,
I hear the Father of the Ancient Men.

`Selfish Father of Men!
Cruel, jealous, selfish Fear!
Can delight,
Chain'd in night,
The virgins of youth and morning bear?

`Does spring hide its joy
When buds and blossoms grow?
Does the sower
Sow by night,

Or the ploughman in darkness plough?

`Break this heavy chain
That does freeze my bones around.
Selfish! vain!
Eternal bane!
That free Love with bondage bound.'

NURSE'S SONG

When the voices of children are heard on the green
And whisp'rings are in the dale,
The days of my youth rise fresh in my mind,
My face turns green and pale.

Then come home, my children, the sun is gone down,
And the dews of night arise;
Your spring and your day are wasted in play,
And your winter and night in disguise.

THE FLY

Little Fly,
Thy summer's play
My thoughtless hand
Has brush'd away.

Am not I
A fly like thee?

Or art not thou
A man like me?

For I dance,
And drink, and sing,
Till some blind hand
Shall brush my wing.

If thought is life
And strength and breath,
And the want
Of thought is death;

Then am I
A happy fly,
If I live
Or if I die.

THE TIGER

Tiger! Tiger! burning bright
In the forests of the night,
What immortal hand or eye
Could frame thy fearful symmetry?

In what distant deeps or skies
Burnt the fire of thine eyes?
On what wings dare he aspire?

What the hand dare seize the fire?

And what shoulder, and what art,
Could twist the sinews of thy heart?
And when thy heart began to beat,
What dread hand? and what dread feet?

What the hammer? what the chain?
In what furnace was thy brain?
What the anvil? what dread grasp
Dare its deadly terrors clasp?

When the stars threw down their spears,
And water'd heaven with their tears,
Did he smile his work to see?
Did he who made the Lamb make thee?

Tiger! Tiger! burning bright
In the forests of the night,
What immortal hand or eye,
Dare frame thy fearful symmetry?

THE LITTLE GIRL LOST

In futurity
I prophetic see
That the earth from sleep
(Grave the sentence deep)

Shall arise and seek
For her Maker meek;
And the desert wild
Become a garden mild.

In the southern clime,
Where the summer's prime
Never fades away,
Lovely Lyca lay.

Seven summers old
Lovely Lyca told;
She had wander'd long
Hearing wild birds' song.

`Sweet sleep, come to me
Underneath this tree.
Do father, mother, weep?
Where can Lyca sleep?

`Lost in desert wild
Is your little child.
How can Lyca sleep
If her mother weep?

`If her heart does ache
Then let Lyca wake;

If my mother sleep,
Lyca shall not weep.

`Frowning, frowning night,
O'er this desert bright,
Let thy moon arise
While I close my eyes.'

Sleeping Lyca lay
While the beasts of prey,
Come from caverns deep,
View'd the maid asleep.

The kingly lion stood,
And the virgin view'd,
Then he gamboll'd round
O'er the hallow'd ground.

Leopards, tigers, play
Round her as she lay,
While the lion old
Bow'd his mane of gold

And her bosom lick,
And upon her neck
From his eyes of flame
Ruby tears there came;

While the lioness
Loos'd her slender dress,
And naked they convey'd
To caves the sleeping maid.

THE LITTLE GIRL FOUND

All the night in woe
Lyca's parents go
Over valleys deep,
While the deserts weep.

Tired and woe-begone,
Hoarse with making moan,
Arm in arm seven days
They trac'd the desert ways.

Seven nights they sleep
Among shadows deep,
And dream they see their child
Starv'd in desert wild. .

Pale, thro' pathless ways
The fancied image strays
Famish'd, weeping, weak,
With hollow piteous shriek.

Rising from unrest,
The trembling woman prest

With feet of weary woe:
She could no further go.

In his arms he bore
Her, arm'd with sorrow sore;
Till before their way
A couching lion lay.

Turning back was vain:
Soon his heavy mane
Bore them to the ground.
Then he stalk'd around,

Smelling to his prey;
But their fears allay
When he licks their hands,
And silent by them stands.

They look upon his eyes
Fill'd with deep surprise;
And wondering behold
A spirit arm'd in gold.

On his head a crown;
On his shoulders down
Flow'd his golden hair.
Gone was all their care.

`Follow me,' he said;
`Weep not for the maid;
In my palace deep
Lyca lies asleep.'

Then they followèd
Where the vision led,
And saw their sleeping child
Among tigers wild.

To this day they dwell
In a lonely dell;
Nor fear the wolfish howl
Nor the lions' growl.

THE COLD AND THE PEBBLE

`Love seeketh hot itself to please,
Nor for itself hath any care,
But for another gives its ease,
And builds a Heaven in Hell's despair.'

So sung a little Clod of Clay,
Trodden with the cattle's feet,
But a Pebble of the brook
Warbled out these metres meet:

`Love seeketh only Self to please,
To bind another to its delight,

Joys in another's loss of ease,
And builds a Hell in Heaven's despite.'

THE LITTLE VAGABOND

But the Ale-house is healthy and pleasant and warm;
Besides I can tell where I am used well,
Such usage in Heaven will never do well.

But if at the Church they would give us some ale,
And a pleasant fire our souls to regale,
We'd sing and we'd pray all the livelong day,
Nor ever once wish from the Church to stray.

Then the Parson might preach, and drink, and sing,
And we'd be as happy as birds in the spring;
And modest Dame Lurch, who is always at church,
Would not have bandy children, nor fasting, nor birch.

And God, like a father, rejoicing to see
His children as pleasant and happy as He,
Would have no more quarrel with the Devil or the barrel,
But kiss him, and give him both drink and apparel.

HOLY THURSDAY

Is this a holy thing to see
In a rich and fruitful land,

Babes reduc'd to misery,
Fed with cold and usurous hand?

Is that trembling cry a song?
Can it be a song of joy?
And so many children poor?
It is a land of poverty!

And their sun does never shine,
And their fields are bleak and bare,
And their ways are fill'd with thorns:
It is eternal winter there.

For where'er the sun does shine,
And where'er the rain does fall,
Babe can never hunger there,
Nor poverty the mind appal.

A POISON TREE

I was angry with my friend:
I told my wrath, my wrath did end.
I was angry with my foe:
I told it not, my wrath did grow.

And I water'd it in fears,
Night and morning with my tears;
And I sunnèd it with smiles,

And with soft deceitful wiles.

And it grew both day and night,
Till it bore an apple bright;
And my foe beheld it shine,
And he knew that it was mine,

And into my garden stole
When the night had veil'd the pole:
In the morning glad I see
My foe outstretch'd beneath the tree.

THE ANGEL

I dreamt a dream! what can it mean?
And that I was a maiden Queen,
Guarded by an Angel mild:
Witless woe was ne'er beguil'd!

And I wept both night and day,
And he wip'd my tears away,
And I wept both day and night,
And hid from him my heart's delight.

So he took his wings and fled;
Then the morn blush'd rosy red;
I dried my tears, and arm'd my fears
With ten thousand shields and spears.

Soon my Angel came again:
I was arm'd, he came in vain;
For the time of youth was fled,
And grey hairs were on my head

THE SICK ROSE

O Rose, thou art sick!
The invisible worm,
That flies in the night,
In the howling storm,

Has found out thy bed
Of crimson joy;
And his dark secret love
Does thy life destroy.

TO TIRZAH

Whate'er is born of mortal birth
Must be consumèd with the earth,
To rise from generation free:
Then what have I to do with thee?

The sexes sprung from shame and pride,
Blow'd in the morn; in evening died;
But Mercy chang'd death into sleep;
The sexes rose to work and weep.

Thou, Mother of my mortal part,
With cruelty didst mould my heart,
And with false self-deceiving tears
Didst bind my nostrils, eyes, and ears;

Didst close my tongue in senseless clay,
And me to mortal life betray:
The death of Jesus set me free:
Then what have I to do with thee?

THE VOICE OF THE ANCIENT BARD

Youth of delight, come hither,
And see the opening morn,
Image of truth new-born.
Doubt is fled, and clouds of reason,
Dark disputes and artful teasing.

Folly is an endless maze,
Tangled roots perplex her ways.
How many have fallen there!
They stumble all night over bones of the dead,
And feel they know not what but care,
And wish to lead others, when they should be led.

MY PRETTY ROSE-TREE

A flower was offer'd to me,
Such a flower as May never bore;
But I said `I've a pretty Rose-tree,'
And I passèd the sweet flower o'er.

Then I went to my pretty Rose-tree,
To tend her by day and by night,
But my Rose turn'd away with jealousy,
And her thorns were my only delight.

AH! SUN-FLOWER

Ah, Sun-flower! weary of time,
Who countest the steps of the sun;
Seeking after that sweet golden clime,
Where the traveller's journey is done;

Where the Youth pined away with desire,
And the pale Virgin shrouded in snow,
Arise from their graves, and aspire
Where my Sun-flower wishes to go.

THE LILY

The modest Rose puts forth a thorn,
The humble Sheep a threat'ning horn;

While the Lily white shall in love delight,
Nor a thorn, nor a threat, stain her beauty bright.

THE GARDEN OF LOVE

I went to the Garden of Love,
And saw what I never had seen:
A Chapel was built in the midst,
Where I used to play on the green.

And the gates of this Chapel were shut,
And `Thou shalt not 'writ over the door;
So I turn'd to the Garden of Love
That so many sweet flowers bore;

And I saw it was fillèd with graves,
And tomb-stones where flowers should be;
And priests in black gowns were walking their rounds,
And binding with briars my joys and desires.

A LITTLE BOY LOST

`Nought loves another as itself,
Nor venerates another so,
Nor is it possible to Thought
A greater than itself to know:

`And, Father, how can I love you
Or any of my brothers more?

I love you like the little bird
That picks up crumbs around the door.'
The Priest sat by and heard the child,

In trembling zeal he seiz'd his hair:
He led him by his little coat,
And all admir'd the priestly care.
And standing on the altar high,

`Lo! what a fiend is here,' said he,
`One who sets reason up for judge
Of our most holy Mystery.'
The weeping child could not be heard,

The weeping parents wept in vain;
They stripp'd him to his little shirt,
And bound him in an iron chain;
And burn'd him in a holy place,

Where many had been burn'd before:
The weeping parents wept in vain.
Are such things done on Albion's shore?

INFANT SORROW

My mother groan'd, my father wept,
Into the dangerous world I leapt;
Helpless, naked, piping loud,

Like a fiend hid in a cloud.

Struggling in my father's hands,
Striving against my swaddling-bands,
Bound and weary, I thought best
To sulk upon my mother's breast.

THE SCHOOLBOY

I love to rise in a summer morn
When the birds sing on every tree;
The distant huntsman winds his horn,
And the skylark sings with me.

O! what sweet company.
But to go to school in a summer morn,
O! it drives all joy away;
Under a cruel eye outworn,
The little ones spend the day
In sighing and dismay.

Ah! then at times I drooping sit,
And spend many an anxious hour,
Nor in my book can I take delight,
Nor sit in learning's bower,
Worn thro' with the dreary shower.

How can the bird that is born for joy
Sit in a cage and sing?

How can a child, when fears annoy,
But droop his tender wing,
And forget his youthful spring?

O! father and mother, if buds are nipp'd
And blossoms blown away,
And if the tender plants are stripp'd
Of their joy in the springing day,
By sorrow and care's dismay,
How shall the summer arise in joy,
Or the summer fruits appear?

Or how shall we gather what griefs destroy,
Or bless the mellowing year,
When the blasts of winter appear?

LONDON

I wander thro' each charter'd street,
Near where the charter'd Thames does flow,
And mark in every face I meet
Marks of weakness, marks of woe.

In every cry of every Man,
In every Infant's cry of fear,
In every voice, in every ban,
The mind-forg'd manacles I hear.

How the chimney-sweeper's cry
Every black'ning church appals;
And the hapless soldier's sigh
Runs in blood down palace walls.

But most thro' midnight streets I hear
How the youthful harlot's curse
Blasts the new-born infant's tear,
And blights with plagues the marriage hearse.

A LITTLE GIRL LOST

Children of the future age,
Reading this indignant page,
Know that in a former time,
Love, sweet Love, was thought a crime!

In the Age of Gold,
Free from winter's cold,
Youth and maiden bright
To the holy light,
Naked in the sunny beams delight.

Once a youthful pair,
Fill'd with softest care,
Met in garden bright
Where the holy light
Had just remov'd the curtains of the night.

There, in rising day,
On the grass they play;
Parents were afar,
Strangers came not near,
And the maiden soon forgot her fear.

Tired with kisses sweet,
They agree to meet
When the silent sleep
Waves o'er heaven's deep,
And the weary tired wanderers weep.

To her father white
Came the maiden bright;
But his loving look,
Like the holy book,
All her tender limbs with terror shook.

`Ona! pale and weak!
To thy father speak:
O! the trembling fear.
O! the dismal care,
That shakes the blossoms of my hoary hair!'

THE CHIMNEY-SWEEPER

A little black thing among the snow,
Crying `'weep! 'weep!' in notes of woe!

`Where are thy father and mother, say?'- -
`They are both gone up to the Church to pray
`Because I was happy upon the heath,
And smil'd among the winter's snow,
They clothèd me in the clothes of death,
And taught me to sing the notes of woe.

`And because I am happy and dance and sing,
They think they have done me no injury,
And are gone to praise God and His Priest and King,
Who make up a Heaven of our misery.'

THE HUMAN ABSTRACT

Pity would be no more
If we did not make somebody poor;
And Mercy no more could be
If all were as happy as we.
And mutual fear brings peace,
Till the selfish loves increase;
Then Cruelty knits a snare,
And spreads his baits with care.
He sits down with holy fears,
And waters the ground with tears;
Then Humility takes its root
Underneath his foot.
Soon spreads the dismal shade
Of Mystery over his head;

And the caterpillar and fly
Feed on the Mystery.
And it bears the fruit of Deceit,
Ruddy and sweet to eat;
And the raven his nest has made
In its thickest shade.
The Gods of the earth and sea
Sought thro' Nature to find this tree;
But their search was all in vain:
There grows one in the Human brain.

APPENDIX TO THE SONGS OF INNOCENCE AND OF EXPERIENCE

A Divine Image
Cruelty has a human heart,
And Jealousy a human face;
Terror the human form divine,
And Secrecy the human dress.
The human dress is forgèd iron,
The human form a fiery forge,
The human face a furnace seal'd,
The human heart its hungry gorge.

THEL'S MOTTO

Does the Eagle know what is in the pit?
Or wilt thou go ask the Mole:
Can Wisdom be put in a silver rod?
Or Love in a golden bowl?

I

The daughters of Mne Seraphim led round
their sunny flocks,
All but the youngest: she in paleness
sought the secret air.
To fade away like morning beauty from her mortal day:
Down by the river of Adona her soft voice is heard;
And thus her gentle lamentation falls like morning dew.

O life of this our spring! why fades
the lotus of the water?
Why fade these children of the spring?
born but to smile & fall.
Ah! Thel is like a watry bow, and like a parting cloud,
Like a reflection in a glass: like shadows in the water
Like dreams of infants, like a smile
upon an infants face.
Like the doves voice, like transient day,

like music in the air:
Ah! gentle may I lay me down and gentle rest my head.
And gentle sleep the sleep of death,
and gently hear the voice
Of him that walketh in the garden in the evening time.

The Lilly of the valley breathing in the humble grass
Answerd the lovely maid and said: I am a watry weed,
And I am very small and love to dwell in lowly vales:
So weak the gilded butterfly scarce perches on my head
Yet I am visited from heaven and he that smiles on all
Walks in the valley,
and each morn over me spreads his hand
Saying, rejoice thou humble grass,
thou new-born lily flower.
Thou gentle maid of silent valleys
and of modest brooks:
For thou shall be clothed in light,
and fed with morning manna:
Till summers heat melts thee beside
the fountains and the springs
To flourish in eternal vales: they
why should Thel complain.
Why should the mistress of the vales of Har,
utter a sigh.

She ceasd & smild in tears, then sat down
in her silver shrine.

Thel answerd, O thou little virgin of the peaceful valley.
Giving to those that cannot crave,
the voiceless, the o'er tired

The breath doth nourish the innocent lamb,
he smells the milky garments
He crops thy flowers while thou
sittest smiling in his face,
Wiping his mild and meekin mouth from
all contagious taints.
Thy wine doth purify the golden honey; thy perfume.
Which thou dost scatter on every little blade of grass
that springs
Revives the milked cow,
& tames the fire-breathing steed.
But Thel is like a faint cloud kindled at the rising sun:
I vanish from my pearly throne,
and who shall find my place.

Queen of the vales the Lily answered,
ask the tender cloud,
And it shall tell thee why it glitters in the morning sky.
And why it scatters its bright beauty thro the humid air.
Descend O little cloud & hover before the eyes of Thel.

The Cloud descended and the Lily
bowd her modest head:
And went to mind her numerous
charge among the verdant grass.

II

O little Cloud the virgin said, I charge thee to tell me
Why thou complainest now when
in one hour thou fade away:
Then we shall seek thee but not find:
ah Thel is like to thee.

I pass away, yet I complain,
and no one hears my voice.

The Cloud then shewd his golden
head & his bright form emerg'd.
Hovering and glittering on the air
before the face of Thel.

O virgin know'st thou not our steeds
drink of the golden springs
Where Luvah doth renew his horses:
lookst thou on my youth.
And fearest thou because I vanish
and am seen no more.
Nothing remains; O maid I tell thee, when I pass away.
It is to tenfold life, to love, to peace, and raptures holy:
Unseen descending, weigh my light
wings upon balmy flowers:
And court the fair eyed dew,
to take me to her shining tent
The weeping virgin, trembling
kneels before the risen sun.
Till we arise link'd in a golden band and never part:
But walk united bearing food to all our tender flowers.

Dost thou O little cloud? I fear that I am not like thee:
For I walk through the vales of Har,
and smell the sweetest flowers:
But I feed not the little flowers:
I hear the warbling birds,
But I feed not the warbling birds,
they fly and seek their food:

But Thel delights in these no more because I fade away
And all shall say, without a use
this shining women liv'd,
Or did she only live to be at death the food of worms.

The Cloud reclind upon his airy
throne and answerd thus.

Then if thou art the food of worms,
O virgin of the skies,
How great thy use, how great thy blessing,
every thing that lives.
Lives not alone nor or itself: fear not and I will call,
The weak worm from its lowly bed,
and thou shalt hear its voice.
Come forth worm and the silent valley,
to thy pensive queen.

The helpless worm arose and sat upon the Lillys leaf,
And the bright Cloud saild on,
to find his partner in the vale.

III

Then Thel astonish'd view'd the
Worm upon its dewy bed.

Art thou a Worm? image of weakness.
art thou but a Worm?
I see thee like an infant wrapped in the Lillys leaf;
Ah weep not little voice, thou can'st not speak,
but thou can'st weep:
Is this a Worm? I see they lay helpless & naked: weeping

And none to answer, none to cherish thee
with mothers smiles.

The Clod of Clay heard the Worms voice &
rais'd her pitying head:
She bowd over the weeping infant, and her life exhald
In milky fondness,
then on Thel she fix'd her humble eyes

O beauty of the vales of Har, we live not for ourselves,
Thou seest me the meanest thing, and so I am indeed:
My bosom of itself is cold, and of itself is dark,

But he that loves the lowly, pours his oil upon my head
And kisses me, and binds his nuptial
bands around my breast.
And says; Thou mother of my children,
I have loved thee
And I have given thee a crown that none can take away.
But how this is sweet maid,
I know not, and I cannot know
I ponder, and I cannot ponder; yet I live and love.

The daughter of beauty wip'd her
pitying tears with her white veil,
And said, Alas! I knew not this,
and therefore did I weep:
That God would love a Worm I knew,
and punish the evil foot
That wilful bruis'd its helpless form:
but that he cherish'd it
With milk and oil I never knew,

and therefore did I weep,
And I complaind in the mild air, because I fade away.
And lay me down in thy cold bed,
and leave my shining lot.

Queen of the vales, the matron Clay answered:
I heard thy sighs.
And all thy moans flew o'er my roof,
but I have call'd them down:
Wilt thou O Queen enter my house,
tis given thee to enter,
And to return: fear nothing, enter with thy virgin feet.

IV

The eternal gates terrific porter lifted the northern bar:
Thel enter'd in & saw the secrets of the land unknown;
She saw the couches of the dead,
& where the fibrous roots
Of every heart on earth infixes deep its restless twists:
A land of sorrows & of tears
where never smile was seen.

She wandered in the land of clouds
thro' valleys dark, listning
Dolors & lamentations: waiting oft
beside the dewy grave
She stood in silence, listning to
the voices of the ground,
Till to her own grave plot she came,
& there she sat down.
And heard this voice of sorrow
breathed from the hollow pit.

Why cannot the Ear be closed to its own destruction?
Or the glistening Eye to the poison of a smile!
Why are Eyelids stord with arrows ready drawn,
Where a thousand fighting men in ambush lie!
Or an Eye of gifts & graces showring fruits
& coined gold!

Why a Tongue impress'd with honey from every wind?
Why an Ear, a whirlpool fierce to draw creations in?
Why a Nostril wide inhaling terror trembling & affright
Why a tender curb upon the youthful burning boy?
Why a little curtain of flesh on the bed of our desire?

The Virgin started from her seat, & with a shriek,
Fled back unhinderd till she came into the vales of Har

A PROPHECY

The Guardian Prince of Albion burns
in his nightly tent:
Sullen fires across the Atlantic glow to America's shore,
Piercing the souls of warlike men
who rise in silent night.
Washington, Franklin, Paine, and Warren, Gates,
Hancock, and Green
Meet on the coast glowing with blood
from Albion's fiery Prince.

Washington spoke: 'Friends of America!

look over the Atlantic sea;
A bended bow is lifted in Heaven,
and a heavy iron chain
Descends, link by link, from Albion's
cliffs across the sea, to bind
Brothers and sons of America;
till our faces pale and yellow,
Heads depress'd, voices weak,
eyes downcast, hands work-bruis'd,
Feet bleeding on the sultry sands,
and the furrows of the whip
Descend to generations, that in future times forget.'

The strong voice ceas'd; for a terrible blast swept
over the heaving sea:
The eastern cloud rent: on his cliffs stood
Albion's wrathful Prince,
A dragon form, clashing his scales:
at midnight he arose,
And flam'd red meteo 1000 rs round the land of
Albion beneath;
His voice, his locks, his awful shoulders,
and his glowing eyes
Appear to the Americans upon the cloudy night.

Solemn heave the Atlantic waves between
the gloomy nations,
Swelling, belching from its deeps red
clouds and raging fires.
Albion is sick! America faints! Enrag'd the Zenith grew.
As human blood shooting its veins
all round the orbed heaven,
Red rose the clouds from the Atlantic
in vast wheels of blood,

And in the red clouds rose a
Wonder o'er the Atlantic sea --
Intense! naked! a Human fire,
fierce glowing, as the wedge
Of iron heated in the furnace;
his terrible limbs were fire,
With myriads of cloudy terrors,
banners dark, and towers
Surrounded: heat but not light went thro'
the murky atmosphere.
The King of England looking westward
trembles at the vision.

Albion's Angel stood beside the Stone of Night, and saw
The Terror like a comet, or more like the planet red,
That once enclos'd the terrible
wandering comets in its sphere.
Then, Mars, thou wast our centre,
and the planets three flew round
Thy crimson disk; so, ere the
Sun was rent from thy red sphere,
The Spectre glow'd, his horrid length
staining the temple long
With beams of blood; and thus a voice came forth,
and shook the temple:--

`The morning comes, the night decays,
the watchmen leave their stations;
The grave is burst, the spices shed,
the linen wrapped up;
The bones of death, the cov'ring clay, the sinews
shrunk and dry'd
Reviving shake, inspiring move, breathing, awakening,
Spring like redeemed captives,

when their bonds and bars are burst
Let the slave grinding at the mill run out into the field,
Let him look up into the heavens
and laugh in the bright air;
Let the enchained soul, shut up in
darkness and in sighing,
Whose face has never seen a smile
in thirty weary years,
Rise and look out; his chains are loose,
his dungeon doors are open;
And let his wife and children return from the
oppressor's scourge.
They look behind at every step,
and believe it is a dream,
Singing: "The Sun has left his blackness,
and has found a fresher morning,
And the fair Moon rejoices in
the clear and cloudless night;
For Empire is no more, and now
the Lion and Wolf shall cease." '

In thunders ends the voice.
Then Albion's Angel wrathful burnt
Beside the Stone of Night; and,
like the Eternal Lion's howl
In famine and war, reply'd:
`Art thou not Orc, who serpent-form'd
Stands at the gate of Enitharmon to devour her
children?
Blasphemous Demon, Antichrist, hater of Dignities,
Lover of wild rebellion, and transgressor of God's Law,
Why dost thou come to Angel's
eyes in this terrific form?'

The Terror answer'd:
`I am Orc, wreath'd round the accursed tree:
The times are ended; shadows pass,
the morning 'gins to break;
The fiery joy, that Urizen perverted to ten commands,
What night he led the starry
hosts thro' the wide wilderness,
That stony Law I stamp to dust;
and scatter Religion abroad
To the four winds as a torn book,
and none shall gather the leaves;
But they shall rot on desert sands,
and consume in bottomless deeps,
To make the deserts blossom,
and the deeps shrink to their fountains,
And to renew the fiery joy, and burst the stony roof;
That pale religious lechery, seeking Virginity,
May find it in a harlot, and in coarse-clad honesty
The undefil'd, tho' ravish'd in
her cradle night and morn;
For everything that lives is holy, life delights in life;
Because the soul of sweet delight can never be defil'd.
Fires enwrap the earthly globe,
yet Man is not consum'd;
Amidst the lustful fires he walks;
his feet become like brass,
His knees and thighs like silver,
and his breast and head like gold.

`Sound! sound! my loud war-trumpets,
and alarm my Thirteen Angels!
Loud howls the Eternal Wolf!
the Eternal Lion lashes his tail!
America is dark'ned;

and my punishing Demons, terrified,
Crouch howling before their caverns deep,
like skins dry'd in the wind.
They cannot smite the wheat,
nor quench the fatness of the earth;
They cannot smite with sorrows, nor subdue the plough and spade;
They cannot wall the city,
nor moat round the castle of princes;
They cannot bring the stubbed oak
to overgrow the hills;
For terrible men stand on the shores,
and in their robes I see
Children take shelter from the lightnings:
there stands Washington,
And Paine, and Warren,
with their foreheads rear'd toward the East--
But clouds obscure my aged sight.
A vision from afar!
Sound! sound! my loud war-trumpets,
and alarm my Thirteen Angels!
Ah, vision from afar!
Ah, rebel form that rent the ancient
Heavens! Eternal Viper self-renew'd, rolling in clouds,
I see thee in thick clouds
and darkness on America's shore,
Writhing in pangs of abhorred birth;
red flames the crest rebellious
And eyes of death; the harlot womb, oft opened in vain,
Heaves in enormous circles: now
the times are return'd upon thee,
Devourer of thy parent,
now thy unutterable torment renews.
Sound! sound! my loud war-trumpets,

and alarm my Thirteen Angels!
Ah, terrible birth! a young one bursting!
Where is the weeping mouth,
And where the mother's milk?
Instead, those ever-hissing jaws
And parched lips drop with fresh gore:
now roll thou in the clouds;
Thy mother lays her length outstretch'd upon
the shore beneath.
Sound! sound! my loud war-trumpets,
and alarm my Thirteen Angels!
Loud howls the Eternal Wolf! the Eternal Lion lashes
his tail!'

Thus wept the Angel voice,
and as he wept the terrible blasts
Of trumpets blew a loud alarm across the Atlantic deep.
No trumpets answer; no reply of clarions or of fifes:
Silent the Colonies remain and refuse the loud alarm.

On those vast shady hills between
America and Albion's shore,
Now barr'd out by the Atlantic sea,
call'd Atlantean hills,
Because from their bright summits you
may pass to the Golden World,
An ancient palace, archetype of mighty Emperies,
Rears its immortal pinnacles, built in the forest of God
By Ariston, the King of Beauty, for his stolen bride.

Here on their magic seats the
Thirteen Angels sat perturb'd,
For clouds from the Atlantic hover o'er the solemn roof.

Fiery the Angels rose,
and as they rose deep thunder roll'd
Around their shores,
indignant burning with the fires of Orc;
And Boston's Angel cried aloud as
they flew thro' the dark night.

He cried: `Why trembles honesty; and, like a murderer,
Why seeks he refuge from the
frowns of his immortal station?
Must the generous tremble,
and leave his joy to the idle, to the pestilence
That mock him? Who commanded this?
What God? What Angel?
To keep the gen'rous from
experience till the ungenerous
Are unrestrain'd performers of the energies of nature;
Till pity is become a trade, and generosity a science
That men get rich by;
and the sandy desert is giv'n to the strong?
What God is he writes laws of peace,
and clothes him in a tempest?
What pitying Angel lusts for tears,
and fans himself with sighs?
What crawling villain preaches
abstinence and wraps himself
In fat of lambs? No more I follow,
no more obedience pay!'

So cried he, rending off his robe
and throwing down his sceptre
In sight of Albion's Guardian;
and all the Thirteen Angels
Rent off their robes to the hungry wind,

and threw their golden sceptres
Down on the land of America;
indignant they descended

Headlong from out their heav'nly heights,
descending s 1000 wift as fires
Over the land; naked and flaming
are their lineaments seen
In the deep gloom; by Washington
and Paine and Warren they stood;
And the flame folded, roaring fierce
within the pitchy night,
Before the Demon red, who burnt towards America,
In black smoke, thunders, and loud winds,
rejoicing in its terror,
Breaking in smoky wreaths from the wild deep,
and gath'ring thick
In flames as of a furnace on
the land from North to South,
What time the Thirteen Governors,
that England sent, convene
In Bernard's house.
The flames cover'd the land;
they rouse; they cry;
Shaking their mental chains,
they rush in fury to the sea
To quench their anguish;
at the feet of Washington down fall'n
They grovel on the sand and writhing lie, while all
The British soldiers thro' the Thirteen States sent up a
howl
Of anguish, threw their swords
and muskets to the earth, and run
From their encampments and dark castles,

seeking where to hide
From the grim flames, and from the visions of Orc,
in sight
Of Albion's Angel; who, enrag'd,
his secret clouds open'd
From North to South,
and burnt outstretch'd on wings of wrath, cov'ring
The eastern sky,
spreading his awful wings across the heavens.
Beneath him roll'd his num'rous hosts,
all Albion's Angels camp'd
Darken'd the Atlantic mountains;
and their trumpets shook the valleys,
Arm'd with diseases of the earth to cast upon the Abyss
--
Their numbers forty millions,
must'ring in the eastern sky.

In the flames stood and view'd
the armies drawn out in the sky,
Washington, Franklin, Paine,
and Warren, Allen, Gates, and Lee,
And heard the voice of Albion's Angel give the
thunderous command;
His plagues, obedient to his voice,
flew forth out of their clouds,
Falling upon America, as a storm to cut them off,
As a blight cuts the tender
corn when it begins to appear.
Dark is the heaven above, and
cold and hard the earth beneath:
And, as a plague-wind, fill'd with insects,
cuts off man and beast,
And, as a sea o'erwhelms a land in

the day of an earthquake,
Fury, rage, madness, in a wind swept through America;
And the red flames of Orc,
that folded roaring, fierce, around
The angry shores; and the fierce rushing of th'
inhabitants together!
The citizens of New York
close their books and lock their chests;
The mariners of Boston drop their anchors and unlade;
The scribe of Pennsylvania
casts his pen upon the earth;

The builder of Virginia throws his
hammer down in fear.

Then had America been lost,
o'erwhelm'd by the Atlantic,
And Earth had lost another portion of the Infinite;
But all rush together in the night in wrath
and raging fire.
The red fires rag'd! The plagues recoil'd!
Then roll'd they back with fury
On Albion's Angels: then the
Pestilence began in streaks of red
Across the limbs of Albion's Guardian;
the spotted plague smote Bristol's,
And the Leprosy London's Spirit,
sickening all their bands:
The millions sent up a howl of anguish
and threw off their hammer'd mail,
And cast their swords and spears to earth,
and stood, a naked multitude:
Albion's Guardian writhed in torment
on the eastern sky,

Pale, quiv'ring toward the brain
his glimmering eyes, teeth chattering,
Howling and shuddering, his legs quivering, convuls'd
each muscle and sinew:
Sick'ning lay London's Guardian,
and the ancient mitred York,
Their heads on snowy hills, their
ensigns sick'ning in the sky.

The plagues creep on the burning winds,
driven by flames of Orc,
And by the fierce Americans rushing
together in the night,
Driven o'er the Guardians of Ireland,
and Scotland and Wales.
They, spotted with plagues, forsook the frontiers;
and their banners, sear'd
With fires of hell, deform their ancient
Heavens with shame and woe.
Hid in his caves the Bard of Albion
felt the enormous plagues,
An a88 d a cowl of flesh grew o'er his head,
and scales on his back and ribs;
And, rough with black scales, all his
Angels fright their ancient heavens.
The doors of marriage are open, and the Priests,
in rustling scales,
Rush into reptile coverts, hiding from the fires of Orc,
That play around the golden roofs
in wreaths of fierce desire,
Leaving the Females naked
and glowing with the lusts of youth.

For the Female Spirits of the dead,
pining in bonds of religion,
Run from their fetters; reddening,
and in long-drawn arches sitting,
They feel the nerves of youth renew,
and desires of ancient times
Over their pale limbs,
as a vine when the tender grape appears.

Over the hills, the vales,
the cities rage the red flames fierce:
The Heavens melted from North to South;
and Urizen, who sat
Above all heavens, in thunders wrapp'd,
emerg'd his leprous head
From out his holy shrine, his tears in deluge piteous

Falling into the deep sublime;
flagg'd with grey-brow'd snows
And thunderous visages,
his jealous wings wav'd over the deep;
Weeping in dismal howling woe,
he dark descended, howling
Around the smitten bands,
clothed in tears and trembling, shudd'ring, cold.
His stored snows he poured forth, and his icy magazine,
He open'd on the deep, and on the Atlantic sea,
white, shiv'ring;
Leprous his limbs, all over white,
and hoary was his visage;
Weeping in dismal howlings before the stern
Americans,
Hiding the Demon red with clouds
and cold mists from the earth;

Till Angels and weak men twelve years should
govern o'er the strong;
And then their end should come, when
France receiv'd the Demon's light.

Stiff shudderings shook the heav'nly thrones!
France, Spain, and Italy
In terror view'd the bands of Albion,
and the ancient Guardians,
Fainting upon the elements,
smitten with their own plagues!
They slow advance to shut the five gates
of their law-built Heaven,
Filled with blasting fancies and with mildews of despair,
With fierce disease and lust,
unable to stem the fires of Orc,
But the five gates were consum'd, and their bolts and
hinges melted;
And the fierce flames burnt round the heavens,
and round the abodes of men.

VISIONS OF THE DAUGHTERS OF ALBION

THE ARGUMENT

I loved Theotormon,
And I was not ashamed;
I trembled in my virgin fears
And I hid in Leutha's vale!

I plucked Leutha's flower,
And I rose up from the vale;
But the terrible thunders tore
My virgin mantle in twain.

VISIONS

Enslav'd, the Daughters of Albion weep;
a trembling lamentation
Upon their mountains; in their valleys,
sighs toward America.

For the soft soul of America, Oothoon, wander'd in woe
Along the vales of Leutha,
seeking flowers to comfort her;
And thus she spoke to the bright Marigold
of Leutha's vale:-

Art thou a flower? art thou a nymph?
I see thee now a flower,
Now a nymph! I dare not pluck thee from thy dewy bed!

The Golden nymph replied:
`Pluck thou my flower, Oothoon the mild!
Another flower shall spring,
because the soul of sweet delight
Can never pass away.' She ceas'd,
and clos'd her golden shrine.

Then Oothoon pluck'd the flower,
saying: `I pluck thee from thy bed,
Sweet flower,
and put thee here to glow between my breasts;
And thus I turn my face to where my whole soul seeks.'

Over the waves she went
in wing'd exulting swift delight,
And over
Theotormon's reign took her impetuous course.

Bromion rent her with his thunders; on his stormy bed
Lay the faint maid, and soon her woes appall'd his
thunders hoarse.

Bromion spoke:
`Behold this harlot here on Bromion's bed,
And let the jealous dolphins sport around
the lovely maid!
Thy soft American plains are mine,
and mine thy north and south:
Stamp'd with my signet are the swarthy
children of the sun;
They are obedient, they resist not,
they obey the scourge;z
Their daughters worship terrors and obey the violent.
Now thou may'st marry Bromion's harlot,
and protect the child
Of Bromion's rage,
that Oothoon shall put forth in nine moons' time.'

Then storms rent Theotormon's limbs:
he roll'd his waves around,
And folded his black jealous waters
round the adulterate pair.
Bound back to back in Bromion's caves,
terror and meekness dwell:

At entrance Theotormon sits,
wearing the threshold hard
With secret tears; beneath him sound like waves on a desert shore
The voice of slaves beneath the sun,
and children bought with money,
That shiver in religious caves beneath the burning fires
Of lust, that belch incessant
from the summits of the earth.

Oothoon weeps not; she cannot weep,
her tears are locked up;
But she can howl incessant,
writhing her soft snowy limbs,
And calling Theotormon's Eagles
to prey upon her flesh.

`I call with holy voice! Kings of the sounding air,
Rend away this defiled bosom that I may reflect
The image of
Theotormon on my pure transparent breast.'

The Eagles at her call descend
and rend their bleeding prey:
Theotormon severely smiles; her soul reflects the smile,
As the clear spring, muddied with feet of beasts, grows pure and smiles.

The Daughters of Albion hear her woes,
and echo back her sighs.

`Why does my
Theotormon sit weeping upon the threshold,
And Oothoon hovers by his side,
per 1000 suading him in vain?

I cry: Arise, O Theotormon! for the village dog
Barks at the breaking day;
the nightingale has done lamenting;

The lark does rustle in the ripe corn,
and the eagle returns
From nightly prey,
and lifts his golden beak to the pure east,
Shaking the dust from his immortal pinions to awake
The sun that sleeps too long. Arise, my Theotormon!
I am pure,
Because the night is gone that
clos'd me in its deadly black.
They told me that the night and day were all that
I could see;
They told me that I had five senses to enclose me up;
And they enclos'd my infinite
brain into a narrow circle,
And sunk my heart into the Abyss, a red,
round globe, hot burning,
Till all from life I was obliterated and erased.
Instead of morn arises a bright shadow, like an eye
In the eastern cloud; instead of
night a sickly charnel-house,
That Theotormon hears me not.
To him the night and morn
Are both alike; a night of sighs, a morning of fresh tears;
And none but Bromion can hear my lamentations.
'With what sense is it that
the chicken shuns the ravenous hawk?
With what sense does the tame pigeon
measure out the expanse?
With what sense does the bee form cells?

Have not the mouse and frog
Eyes and ears and sense of touch?
Yet are their habitations
And their pursuits as different as their
forms and as their joys.
Ask the wild ass why he refuses burdens,
and the meek camel
Why he loves man. Is it because of eye,
ear, mouth, or skin,
Or breathing nostrils?
No! for these the wolf and tiger have.
Ask the blind worm the secrets of the grave,
and why her spires
Love to curl round the bones of death;
and ask the rav'nous snake
Where she gets poison,
and the wing'd eagle why he loves the sun;
And then tell me the thoughts of man,
that have been hid of old.

'Silent I hover all the night, and all day could be silent,
If Theotormon once would turn
his loved eyes upon me.
How can I be defil'd when I reflect thy image pure?
Sweetest the fruit that the worm feeds on,
and the soul prey'd on by woe,
The new-wash'd lamb ting'd with the village smoke,
and the bright swan
By the red earth of our immortal river.
I bathe my wings,
And I am white and pure to hover round
Theotormon's breast.'

Then Theotormon broke his silence, and he answered:-
- `Tell me what is the night or day
to one o'erflow'd with woe?

Tell me what is a thought,
and of what substance is it made?
Tell me what is a joy, and in what gardens do joys grow?
And in what rivers swim the sorrows?
And upon what mountains
Wave shadows of discontent?
And in what houses dwell the wretched,
Drunken with woe, forgotten,
and shut up from cold despair?
`Tell me where dwell the thoughts,
forgotten till thou call them forth?
Tell me where dwell the joys of old,
and where the ancient loves,
And when will they renew again,
and the night of oblivion past,
That I might traverse times and spaces far remote,
and bring
Comforts into a present sorrow and a night of pain?
Where goest thou,
O thought? to what remote land is thy flight?
If thou returnest to the present moment of affliction,
Wilt thou bring comforts on thy wings,
and dews and honey and balm,
Or poison from the desert wilds,
from the eyes of the envier?'

Then Bromion said,
and shook the cavern with his lamentation:--

`Thou knowest that the ancient trees seen by thine
eyes have fruit;
But knowest thou that trees
and fruits flourish upon the earth
To gratify senses unknown -- trees,
beasts, and birds unknown;
Unknown, not unperceiv'd,
spread in the infinite microscope,
In places yet unvisited by the voyager,
and in worlds
Over another kind of seas,
a 1000 nd in atmospheres unknown?
Ah! are there other wars,
beside the wars of sword and fire?
And are there other sorrows
beside the sorrows of poverty?
And are there other joys
beside the joys of riches and ease?
And is there not one law for both the lion and the ox?
And is there not eternal fire, and eternal chains
To bind the phantoms of existence from eternal life?'

Then Oothoon waited silent
all the day and all the night;
But when the morn arose, her lamentation renew'd;
The Daughters of Albion hear her woes,
and echo back her sighs.

`O Urizen! Creator of men! mistaken Demon of heaven!
Thy joys are tears, thy labour
vain to form men to thine image.
How can one joy absorb another?
Are not different joys
Holy, eternal, infinite? and each joy is a Love.

`Does not the great mouth laugh at a gift,
and the narrow eyelids mock
At the labour that is above payment?
And wilt thou take the ape
For thy counsellor,
or the dog for a schoolmaster to thy children?
Does he who contemns poverty,
and he who turns with abhorrence
From usury feel the same passion,
or are they moved alike?
How can the giver of gifts experience the
delights of the merchant?
How the industrious citizen the pains
of the husbandman?
How different far the fat fed hireling with hollow drum,
Who buys whole corn-fields into wastes,
and sings upon the heath!
How different their eye and ear!
How different the world to them!
With what sense does the parson
claim the labour of the farmer?
What are his nets and gins and traps;
and how does he surround him
With cold floods of abstraction,
and with forests of solitude,
To build him castles and high spires,
where kings and priests may dwell;
Till she who burns with youth,
and knows no fixed lot, is bound
In spells of law to one she loathes?
And must she drag the chain
Of life in weary lust?

Must chilling, murderous thoughts obscure
The clear heaven of her eternal spring;
to bear the wintry rage
Of a harsh terror, driv'n to madness, bound to hold a rod
Over her shrinking shoulders all the day,
and all the night
To turn the wheel of false desire,
and longings that wake her womb
To the abhorred birth of cherubs in the human form,
That live a pestilence and die a meteor,
and are no more;
Till the child dwell with one he hates,
and do the deed he loathes,
And the impure scourge force
his seed into its unripe birth,
Ere yet his eyelids can behold
the arrows of the day?
`Does the whale worship at thy
footsteps as the hungry dog;
Or does he scent the mountain
prey because his nostrils wide
Draw in the ocean?
Does his eye discern the flying cloud
As the raven's eye;
or does he measure the expanse like the vulture?
Does the still spider view
the cliffs where eagles hide their young;
Or does the fly rejoice
because the harvest is brought in?
Does not the eagle scorn the earth,
and despise the treasures beneath?
But the mole knoweth what is there,
and the worm shall tell it thee.
Does not the worm erect a

pillar in the mouldering churchyard
And a palace of eternity in the jaws of
the hungry grave?
Over his porch these words are written:
"Take thy bliss, O Man!
And sweet shall be thy taste,
and sweet thy infant joys renew!"

`Infancy! fearless, lustful, happy, nestling for delight
In laps of pleasure: Innocence! honest, open, seeking
The vigorous joys of morning light,
open to virgin bliss,
Who taught thee modesty, subtil modesty,
child of night and sleep?
When thou awakest wilt thou dissemble
all thy secret joys,
Or wert thou not awake when
all this mystery was disclos'd?
Then com'st thou forth a modest
virgin knowing to dissemble,
With nets found under thy night pillow,
to catch virgin joy
And brand it wit 1000 h the name of whore,
and sell it in the night
In silence, ev'n without a whisper,
and in seeming sleep.
Religious dreams and holy
vespers light thy smoky fires:
Once were thy fires lighted by the eyes of honest morn.
And does my Theotormon seek this hypocrite modesty,
This knowing, artful, secret, fearful,
cautious, trembling hypocrite?
Then is Oothoon a whore indeed!

and all the virgin joys
Of life are harlots;
and Theotormon is a sick man's dream;
And Oothoon is the crafty slave of selfish holiness.
`But Oothoon is not so,
a virgin fill'd with virgin fancies,
Open to joy and to delight wherever beauty appears:
If in the morning sun I find it,
there my eyes are fix'd
In happy copulation; if in evening mild,
wearied with work,
Sit on a bank and draw the pleasures
of this free-born joy.

`The moment of desire! the moment of desire!
The virgin
That pines for man shall awaken
her womb to enormous joys
In the secret shadows of her chamber:
the youth shut up from
The lustful joy shall forget to generate,
and create an amorous image
In the shadows of his curtains
and in the folds of his silent pillow
Are not these the places of religion,
the rewards of continence,
The self-enjoyings of self-denial?
Why dost thou seek religion?
Is it because acts are not lovely
that thou seekest solitude,
Where the horrible darkness is impressed with
reflections of desire?

`Father of Jealousy, be thou accursed from the earth!
Why hast thou taught my
Theotormon this accursed thing,
Till beauty fades from off my shoulders,
darken'd and cast out,
A solitary shadow wailing on the margin of nonentity?

`I cry: Love! Love! Love! happy happy
Love! free as the mountain wind!

Can that be Love, that drinks another
as a sponge drinks water,
That clouds with jealousy his nights,
with weepings all the day,
To spin a web of age around him, grey and hoary, dark;
Till his eyes sicken at the fruit
that hangs before his sight?
Such is self-love that envies all, a creeping skeleton,
With lamplike eyes watching
around the frozen marriage bed!
`But silken nets and traps of adamant will
Oothoon spread,
And catch for thee girls of mild silver,
or of furious gold.
I'll lie beside thee on a bank,
and view their wanton play
In lovely copulation, bliss on bliss, with Theotormon:
Red as the rosy morning, lustful as the first-born beam,
Oothoon shall view his dear delight;
nor e'er with jealous cloud
Come in the heaven of generous love,
nor selfish blightings bring.

`Does the sun walk, in glorious raiment,
on the secret floor
Where the cold miser spreads his gold;
or does the bright cloud drop
On his stone threshold?
Does his eye behold the beam that brings
Expansion to the eye of pity;
or will he bind himself
Beside the ox to thy hard furrow?
Does not that mild beam blot
The bat, the owl, the glowing tiger,
and the king of night?
The sea-fowl takes the wintry
blast for a cov'ring to her limbs,
And the wild snake the pestilence
to adorn him with gems and gold;
And trees, and birds, and beasts,
and men behold their eternal joy.
Arise, you little glancing wings,
and sing your infant joy!
Arise, and drink your bliss,
for everything that lives is holy!'

Thus every morning wails Oothoon;
but Theotormon sits
Upon the margin'd ocean conversing with shadows
dire.

The Daughters of Albion hear her woes,
and echo back her sighs.

THE SONG OF LOS

AFRICA

I Will sing you a song of Los, the Eternal Prophet:
He sung it to four harps, at the tables of Eternity,
In heart-formed Africa.
Urizen faded! Ariston shudder'd!
And thus the Song began;--

Adam stood in the garden of Eden,
And Noah on the mountains of Ararat;
They saw Urizen give his Laws to the Nations
By the hands of the children of Los.

Adam shudder'd! Noah faded!
Black grew the sunny African
When Rintrah gave
Abstract Philosophy to Brahma in the East.
(Night spoke to the Cloud:
`Lo! these Human-form'd spirits, in smiling hypocrisy, war
Against one another; so let them war on,
slaves to the eternal elements.')
Noah shrunk beneath the waters,

Abram fled in fires from Chaldaea;
Moses beheld upon Mount Sinai forms of dark delusion.

To Trismegistus, Palamabron gave an abstract Law;
To Pythagoras, Socrates, and Plato.

Times rolled on o'er all the sons of Har: time after time
Orc on Mount Atlas howl'd, chain'd down with the Chain of Jealousy;
Then Oothoon hover'd over Judah and Jerusalem,
And Jesus heard her voice -- a Man of Sorrows! -- He receiv'd
A Gospel from wretched Theotormon.

The human race began to wither; for the healthy built
Secluded places, fearing the joys of Love,

And the diseased only propagated.
So Antamon call'd up Leutha from her valleys of delight,
And to Mahomet a loose Bible gave;
But in the North, to Odin, Sotha gave a Code of War,
Because of Diralada, thinking to reclaim his joy.
These were the Churches, Hospitals, Castles, Palaces,
Like nets and gins and traps, to catch the joys of Eternity,
And all the rest a desert;
Till, like a dream, Eternity was obliterated and erased,

Since that dread day when Har and Heva fled,
Because their brethren and sisters liv'd in War and Lust;
And, as they fled, they shrunk
Into two narrow doleful forms,
Creeping in reptile flesh upon
The bosom of the ground;
And all the vast of Nature shrunk
Before their shrunken eyes.

Thus the terrible race of Los and Enitharmon gave
Laws and Religions to the sons of Har,
binding them more
And more to Earth, closing and restraining;
Till a Philosophy of Five Senses was complete:
Urizen wept,
and gave it into the hands of Newton and Locke.

Clouds roll heavy upon the Alps round Rousseau
and Voltaire,
And on the mountains of Lebanon
round the deceased Gods
Of Asia, and on the deserts of Africa round
the Fallen Angels.
The Guardian Prince of
Albion burns in his nightly tent.

ASIA

The Kings of Asia heard
The howl rise up from Europe,
And each ran out from his Web,
From his ancient woven Den;
For the darkness of Asia was startled
At the thick-flaming, thought-creating fires of Orc.

And the Kings of Asia stood
And cried in bitterness of soul:--

`Shall not the King call for Famine from the heath,
Nor the Priest for Pestilence from the fen,
To restrain, to dismay, to thin
The inhabitants of mountain and plain,
In the day of full-feeding prosperity
And the night of delicious songs?

Shall not the Counsellor throw his curb
Of Poverty on the laborious,
To fix the price of labour,
To invent allegoric riches?

And the privy admonishers of men
Call for Fires in the City,
For heaps of smoking ruins,
In the night of prosperity and wantonness,

To turn man from his path,
To restrain the child from the womb,
To cut off the bread from the city;
That the remnant may learn to obey,

That the pride of the heart may fail,
That the lust of the eyes may be quench'd,
That the delicate ear in its infancy
May be dull'd, and the nostrils clos'd up,
To teach Mortal Worms the path
That leads from the gates of the Grave?'

Urizen heard them cry,
And his shudd'ring, waving wings
Went enormous above the red flames,
Drawing clouds of despair thro' the Heavens
Of Europe as he went.
And his Books of brass, iron, and gold
Melted over the land as he flew,
Heavy-waving, howling, weeping.

And he stood over Judaea,
And stay'd in his ancient place,
And stretch'd his clouds over Jerusalem;

For Adam, a mouldering skeleton,
Lay bleach'd on the garden of Eden;
And Noah, as white as snow,

On the mountains of Ararat.

Then the thunders of Urizen bellow'd aloud
From his woven darkness above.

Orc, raging in European darkness,
Arose like a pillar of fire above the Alps,
Like a serpent of fiery flame!
The sullen Earth
Shrunk!

Forth from the dead dust, rattling bones to bones
Join. Shaking, convuls'd, the shiv'ring Clay breathes,
And all Flesh naked stands: Fathers and Friends,
Mothers and Infants, Kings and Warriors.

The Grave shrieks with delight, and shakes
Her hollow womb, and clasps the solid stem:
Her bosom swells with wild desire;
And milk and blood and glandous wine
In rivers rush, and shout and dance,
On mountain, dale, and plain.

THE BOOK OF URIZEN

PRELUDIUM

Of the primeval Priest's assum'd power,
When Eternals spurn'd back his Religion,
And gave him a place in the North,
Obscure, shadowy, void, solitary.

Eternals! I hear your call gladly.
Dictate swift winged words, and fear not
To unfold your dark visions of torment.

CHAPTER I

1. Lo, a Shadow of horror is risen
In Eternity! unknown, unprolific,
Self-clos'd, all-repelling. What Demon
Hath form'd this abominable Void,
This soul-shudd'ring Vacuum? Some said
It is Urizen. But unknown, abstracted,
Brooding, secret, the dark Power hid.

2. Times on times he divided, and measur'd
Space by space in his ninefold darkness,
Unseen, unknown; changes appear'd
Like desolate mountains, rifted furious
By the black winds of perturbation.

3. For he strove in battles dire,
In unseen conflictions with Shapes,
Bred from his forsaken wilderness,
Of beast, bird, fish, serpent, and element,
Combustion, blast, vapour, and cloud.

4. Dark, revolving in silent activity,
Unseen in tormenting passions,
An Activity unknown and horrible,
A self-contemplating Shadow,
In enormous labours occupied.
5. But Eternals beheld his vast forests;
Ages on ages he lay, clos'd, unknown,
Brooding, shut in the deep; all avoid
The petrific, abominable Chaos.

6. His cold horrors, silent, dark Urizen
Prepar'd; his ten thousands of thunders,
Rang'd in gloom'd array, stretch out across
The dread world; and the rolling of wheels,
As of swelling seas, sound in his clouds,

In his hills of stor'd snows, in his mountains
Of hail and ice; voices of terror
Are heard, like thunders of autumn,
When the cloud blazes over the harvests.

CHAPTER II

1. Earth was not, nor globes of attraction;
The will of the Immortal expanded
Or contracted his all-flexible senses;
Death was not, but Eternal life sprung.

2. The sound of a trumpet the heavens

Awoke, and vast clouds of blood roll'd
Round the dim rocks of Urizen, so nam'd
That solitary one in Immensity.

3. Shrill the trumpet! and myriads of Eternity
Muster around the bleak deserts,
Now fill'd with clouds, darkness, and waters,
That roll'd perplex'd, lab'ring; and utter'd
Words articulate, bursting in thunders,
That roll'd on the tops of his mountains:--

4. `From the depths of dark solitude, from
The Eternal abode in my Holiness,
Hidden, set apart, in my stern counsels,
Reserv'd for the days of futurity,
I have sought for a joy without pain,
For a solid without fluctuation.
Why will you die, O Eternals?
Why live in unquenchable burnings?
5. `First I fought with the fire, consum'd
Inwards into a deep world within,
A Void immense, wild, dark and deep,
Where nothing was--Nature's wide womb;
And self-balanc'd, stretch'd o'er the void,
I alone, even I! the winds merciless
Bound; but condensing in torrents
They fa 1000 ll and fall; strong I repell'd
The vast waves, and arose on the waters
A wide World of solid obstruction.

6. `Here alone I, in books form'd of metals,
Have written the secrets of Wisdom,
The secrets of dark Contemplation,
By fightings and conflicts dire
With terrible monsters sin-bred,

Which the bosoms of all inhabit--
Seven deadly Sins of the Soul.

7. `Lo! I unfold my darkness, and on
This rock place, with strong hand, the Book
Of Eternal brass, written in my solitude:

8. `Laws of peace, of love, of unity,
Of pity, compassion, forgiveness;
Let each choose one habitation,
His ancient infinite mansion,
One command, one joy, one desire,
One curse, one weight, one measure,
One King, one God, one Law.'

CHAPTER III

1. The voice ended: they saw his pale visage
Emerge from the darkness, his hand
On the rock of Eternity unclasping
The Book of brass. Rage seiz'd the strong--

2. Rage, fury, intense indignation,
In cataracts of fire, blood, and gall,
In whirlwinds of sulphurous smoke,
And enormous forms of energy,
In living creations appear'd,
In the flames of eternal fury.

3. Sund'ring, dark'ning, thund'ring,
Rent away with a terrible crash,
Eternity roll'd wide apart,
Wide asunder rolling;
Mountainous, all around
Departing, departing, departing,
Leaving ruinous fragments of life,

Hanging, frowning cliffs, and, all between,
An Ocean of voidness unfathomable.

4. The roaring fires ran o'er the heav'ns
In whirlwinds and cataracts of blood,
And o'er the dark deserts of Urizen
Fires pour thro' the void, on all sides,
On Urizen's self-begotten armies.

5. But no light from the fires! all was darkness
In the flames of Eternal fury.

6. In fierce anguish and quenchless flames
To the deserts and rocks he ran raging,
To hide; but he could not. Combining,
He dug mountains and hills in vast strength,
He piled them in incessant labour,
In howlings and pangs and fierce madness,
Long periods in burning fires labouring;
Till hoary, and age-broke, and aged,
In despair and the shadows of death

7. And a roof vast, petrific, around
On all sides he fram'd, like a womb,
Where thousands of rivers, in veins
Of blood, pour down the mountains to cool
The eternal fires, beating without
From Eternals; and like a black Globe,
View'd by sons of Eternity, standing
On the shore of the infinite ocean,
Like a human heart, struggling and beating,
The vast world of Urizen appear'd.
8. And Los, round the dark globe of Urizen,
Kept watch for Eternals to confine
The obscure separation alone;

For Eternity stood wide apart,
As the stars are apart from the earth,

9. Los wept, howling around the dark Demon,
And cursing his lot; for in anguish
Urizen was rent from his side,
And a fathomless Void for his feet,
And intense fires for his dwelling.

10. But Urizen, laid in a story sleep,
Unorganiz'd, rent from Eternity.

11. The Eternals said: 'What is this? Death?
Urizen is a clod of clay!'

12. Los howl'd in a dismal stupor,
Groaning, gnashing, groaning,
Till the wrenching apart was healed.

13. But the wrenching of Urizen heal'd not.
Cold, featureless, flesh or clay,
Rifted with direful changes,
He lay in a dreamless night,

14. Till Los rous'd his fires, affrighted
At the formless, unmeasurable Death.

CHAPTER IV

I

1. Los, smitten with astonishment,
Frighten'd at the hurtling bones

2. And at the surging, sulphureous,
Perturbed, immortal, mad raging

3. In whirlwinds, and pitch, and nitre
Round the furious limbs of Los.

4. And Los formed nets and gins,
And threw the nets round about.

5. He watch'd in shudd'ring fear
The dark changes, and bound every change
With rivets of iron and brass.

6. And these were the changes of Urizen:--

II

1. Ages on ages roll'd over him;
In stony sleep ages roll'd over him,
Like a dark waste stretching, changeable,
By earthquakes riv'n, belching sullen fires:
On ages roll'd ages in ghastly
Sick torment; around him in whirlwinds
Of darkness the Eternal Prophet howl'd,
Beating still on his rivets of iron,
Pouring solder of iron; dividing
The horrible night into watches.

2. And Urizen (so his eternal name)
His prolific delight obscur'd more and more,
In dark secrecy hiding in surging
Sulphureous fluid his phantasies.
The Eternal Prophet heav'd the dark bellows,
And turn'd restless the tongs, and the hammer
Incessant beat, forging chains new and new,
Numb'ring with links hours, days, and years.

3. The Eternal mind, bounded, began to roll
Eddies of wrath, ceaseless, round and round,
And the sulphureous foam, surging thick,
Settled, a lake, bright and shining clear,
White as the snow on the mountains cold.

4. Forgetfulness, dumbness, necessity,
In chains of the mind locked up,
Like fetters of ice shrinking together,
Disorganiz'd, rent from Eternity,
Los beat on his fetters of iron;
And heated his furnaces, and pour'd
Iron solder and solder of brass.

5. Restless turn'd the Immortal, enchain'd,
Heaving dolorous, anguish'd, unbearable;
Till a roof, shaggy, wild, enclos'd
In an orb his fountain of thought.

6. In a horrible, dreamful slumber,
Like the linked infernal chain,
A vast Spine writh'd in torment
Upon the winds, shooting pain'd
Ribs, like a bending cavern;
And bones of solidness froze
Over all his nerves of joy--
And a first Age passed over,
And a state of dismal woe.

7. From the caverns of his jointed Spine
Down sunk with fright a red
Round Globe, hot, burning, deep,
Deep down into the Abyss;
Panting, conglobing, trembling,
Shooting out ten thousand branches
Around his solid bones--

And a second Age passed over,
And a state of dismal woe.

8. In harrowing fear rolling round,
His nervous Brain shot branches
Round the branches of his Heart,
On high, into two little orbs,
And fixed in two little caves,
Hiding carefully from the wind,
His Eyes beheld the deep--
And a third Age passed over,
And a state of dismal woe.
9. The pangs of hope began.
In heavy pain, striving, struggling,
Two Ears, in close volutions,
From beneath his orbs of vision
Shot spiring out, and petrified
As they grew--And a fourth Age passed,
And a state of dismal woe.

10. In ghastly torment sick,
Hanging upon the wind,
Two Nostrils bent down to the deep--
And a fifth Age passed over,
And a state of dismal woe.

11. In ghastly torment sick,
Within his ribs bloated round
A craving, hungry Cavern;
Thence aros 1000 e his channell'd Throat,
And, like a red flame, a Tongue
Of thirst and of hunger appear'd--
And a sixth Age passed over,
And a state of dismal woe.

12. Enraged and stifled with torment,
He threw his right Arm to the North,
His left Arm to the South,
Shooting out in anguish deep,
And his Feet stamp'd the nether Abyss
In trembling and howling and dismay--
And a seventh Age passed over,
And a state of dismal woe.

CHAPTER V

1. In terrors Los shrunk from his task:
His great hammer fell from his hand;
His fires beheld, and sickening
Hid their strong limbs in smoke;
For with noises, ruinous, loud,
With hurtlings and clashings and groans,
The Immortal endur'd his chains,
Tho' bound in a deadly sleep.

2. All the myriads of Eternity,
All the wisdom and joy of life
Roll like a sea around him;
Except what his little orbs
Of sight by degrees unfold.

3. And now his Eternal life,
Like a dream, was obliterated.

4. Shudd'ring, the Eternal Prophet smote
With a stroke from his North to South region.
The bellows and hammer are silent now;
A nerveless silence his prophetic voice
Seiz'd; a cold Solitude and dark Void
The Eternal Prophet and Urizen clos'd.

5. Ages on ages roll'd over them,
Cut off from life and light, frozen
Into horrible forms of deformity.
Los suffer'd his fires to decay;
Then he look'd back with anxious desire,
But the Space, undivided by existence,
Struck horror into his soul.

6. Los wept, obscur'd with mourning,
His bosom earthquak'd with sighs;
He saw Urizen, deadly, black,
In his chains bound; and Pity began,

7. In anguish dividing and dividing--
For Pity divides the soul--
In pangs, Eternity on Eternity,
Life in cataracts pour'd down his cliffs.
The Void shrunk the lymph into Nerves,
Wand'ring wide on the bosom of night,
And left a round globe of blood
Trembling upon the Void.
Thus the Eternal Prophet was divided
Before the death image of Urizen;
For in changeable clouds and darkness,
In a winterly night beneath,
The Abyss of Los stretch'd immense;
And now seen, now obscur'd, to the eyes
Of Eternals the visions remote
Of the dark separation appear'd:
As glasses discover Worlds
In the endless Abyss of space,
So the expanding eyes of Immortals
Beheld the dark visions of Los,
And the globe of life-blood trembling.

8. The globe of life-blood trembled,
Branching out into roots,
Fibrous, writhing upon the winds,
Fibres of blood, milk, and tears,
In pangs, Eternity on Eternity.
At length in tears and cries embodied,
A Female form, trembling and pale,
Waves before his deathy face.

9. All Eternity shudder'd at sight
Of the first Female, now separate,
Pale as a cloud of snow,
Waving before the face of Los.

10. Wonder, awe, fear, astonishment
Petrify the Eternal myriads
At the first Female form now separate.
They call'd her Pity, and fled.

11. `Spread a Tent with strong curtains around them!
Let cords and stakes bind in the Void,
That Eternals may no more behold them.'
12. They began to weave curtains of darkness,
They erected large pillars round the Void,
With golden hooks fasten'd in the pillars;
With infinite labour the Eternals
A woof wove, and called it Science.

CHAPTER VI

1. But Los saw the Fem 1000 ale, and pitied;
He embrac'd her; she wept, she refus'd;
In perverse and cruel delight
She fled from his arms, yet he follow'd.

2. Eternity shudder'd when they saw
Man begetting his likeness
On his own Divided Image!

3. A time passed over: the Eternals
Began to erect the tent,
When Enitharmon, sick,
Felt a Worm within her womb.

4. Yet helpless it lay, like a Worm
In the trembling womb,
To be moulded into existence.

5. All day the Worm lay on her bosom;
All night within her womb
The Worm lay till it grew to a Serpent,
With dolorous hissings and poisons
Round Enitharmon's loins folding.

6. Coil'd within Enitharmon's womb
The Serpent grew, casting its scales;
With sharp pangs the hissings began

To change to a grating cry --
Many sorrows and dismal throes,
Many forms of fish, bird, and beast
Brought forth an Infant form
Where was a Worm before.
7. The Eternals their tent finished,
Alarm'd with these gloomy visions,
When Enitharmon, groaning,
Produc'd a Man-Child to the light.

8. A shriek ran thro' Eternity,
And a paralytic stroke,
At the birth of the Human Shadow.

9. Delving earth in his resistless way,
Howling, the Child with fierce flames
Issu'd from Enitharmon.

10. The Eternals closed the tent;
They beat down the stakes, the cords
Stretch'd for a work of Eternity --
No more Los beheld Eternity!

11. In his hands he seiz'd the Infant,
He bathed him in springs of sorrow,
He gave him to Enitharmon.

CHAPTER VII

1. They named the child Orc; he grew,
Fed with milk of Enitharmon.

2. Los awoke her. O sorrow and pain!
A tight'ning girdle grew
Around his bosom. In sobbings
He burst the girdle in twain;
But still another girdle
Oppress'd his bosom. In sobbings

Again he burst it. Again
Another girdle succeeds.
The girdle was form'd by day;
By night was burst in twain.

3. These falling down on the Rock
Into an iron Chain,
In each other link by link lock'd.

4. They took Orc to the top of a mountain.
O how Enitharmon wept!
They chain'd his young limbs to the Rock
With the Chain of Jealousy,
Beneath Urizen's deathful Shadow.

5. The Dead heard the voice of the Child,
And began to awake from sleep;
All things heard the voice of the Child,
And began to awake to life.

6. And Urizen, craving with hunger,
Stung with the odours of Nature,
Explor'd his dens around.

7. He form'd a line and a plummet
To divide the Abyss beneath;
He form'd a dividing rule;

8. He formed scales to weigh,
He formed massy weights;
He formed a brazen quadrant;
He formed golden compasses,
And began to explore the Abyss;
And he planted a garden of fruits.

9. But Los encircled Enitharmon
With fires of Prophecy
From the sight of Urizen and Orc.

10. And she bore an enormous race.

CHAPTER VIII

1. Urizen explor'd his dens,
Mountain, moor, and wilderness,
With a globe of fire lighting his journey --
A fearful journey, annoy'd
By cruel enormities, forms
Of life on his forsaken mountains.

2. And his World teem'd vast enormities,
Fright'ning, faithless, fawning,
Portions of life, similitudes
Of a foot, or a hand, or a head,
Or a heart, or an eye; they swam mischievous,
Dread terrors, delighting in blood!

3. Most Urizen sicken'd to see
His eternal creations appear,
Sons and daughters of sorrow, on mountains,
Weeping, wailing. First Thiriel appear'd,
Astonish'd at his own existence,
Like a man from a cloud born; and Utha,
From the waters emerging, laments;
Grodna rent the deep earth, howling,
Amaz'd; his heavens immense crack
Like the ground parch'd with heat; then Fuzon
Flam'd out, first begotten, last born;
All his Eternal sons in like manner;
His daughters, from green herbs and cattle,
From monsters and worms of the pit.

4. He in darkness clos'd view'd all his race,
And his soul sicken'd! He curs'd
Both sons and daughters; for he saw
That no flesh nor spirit could keep
His iron laws one moment.

5. For he saw that Life liv'd upon Death:
The Ox in the slaughter-house moans;
The Dog at the wintry door;
And he wept, and he called it Pity,
And his tears flowed down on the winds.

6. Cold he wander'd on high, over their Cities,
In weeping and pain and woe;
And wherever he wander'd, in sorrows
Upon the aged Heavens,
A cold Shadow follow'd behind him
Like a spider's web, moist, cold, and dim,
Drawing out from his sorrowing soul,
The dungeon-like heaven dividing,
Wherever the footsteps of Urizen
Walked over the cities in sorrow;
7. Till a Web, dark and cold, throughout all
The tormented element stretch'd
From the sorrows of Urizen's soul.
And the Web is a Female in embryo;
None could break the Web, no wings of fire,

8. So twisted the cords, and so knotted
The meshes, twisted like to the human brain.

9. And all call'd it the Net of Religion.

CHAPTER IX

1. Then the Inhabitants of those Cities
Felt their Nerves change into Marrow,
And hardening Bones began
In swift diseases and torments,
In throbbings and shootings and grindings,

Thro' all the coasts; till weaken'd
The Senses inward rush'd, shrinking
Beneath the dark Net of infection;

2. Till the shrunken eyes, clouded over,
Discern'd not the woven Hypocrisy;
But the streaky slime in their heavens,
Brought together by narrowing perceptions,
Appear'd transparent air; for their eyes
Grew small like the eyes of a man,
And, in reptile forms shrinking together,
Of seven feet stature they remain'd.

3. Six days they shrunk up from existence,
And on the seventh day they rested,
And they bless'd the seventh day, in sick hope,
And forgot their Eternal life.
4. And their Thirty Cities divided
In form of a Human Heart.
No more could they rise at will
In the infinite Void, but bound down
To earth by their narrowing perceptions,
They lived a period of years;
Then left a noisome body
To the jaws of devouring darkness.

5. And their children wept, and built
Tombs in the desolate places,
And form'd Laws of Prudence, and call'd them
The Eternal Laws of God.

6. And the Thirty Cities remain'd,
Surrounded by salt floods, now call'd
Africa: its name was then Egypt.

7. The remaining sons of Urizen
Beheld their brethren shrink together
Beneath the Net of Urizen.
Persuasion was in vain;
For the ears of the inhabitants
Were with 29b er'd and deafen'd and cold,
And their eyes could not discern
Their brethren of other cities.

8. So Fuzon call'd all together
The remaining children of Urizen,
And they left the pendulous earth.
They called it Egypt, and left it.

9. And the salt Ocean rolled englob'd.

~~~
~~~